Books

Historical Western Romance Series

MacLarens of Fire Mountain

Tougher than the Rest, Book One
Faster than the Rest, Book Two
Harder than the Rest, Book Three
Stronger than the Rest, Book Four
Deadlier than the Rest, Book Five
Wilder than the Rest, Book Six

Redemption Mountain

Redemption's Edge, Book One
Wildfire Creek, Book Two
Sunrise Ridge, Book Three
Dixie Moon, Book Four
Survivor Pass, Book Five
Promise Trail, Book Six
Deep River, Book Seven
Courage Canyon, Book Eight
Forsaken Falls, Book Nine
Solitude Gorge, Book Ten
Rogue Rapids, Book Eleven
Angel Peak, Book Twelve
Restless Wind, Book Thirteen
Storm Summit, Book Fourteen, Coming Next in the
Series!

MacLarens of Boundary Mountain

Colin's Quest, Book One,
Brodie's Gamble, Book Two
Quinn's Honor, Book Three
Sam's Legacy, Book Four
Heather's Choice, Book Five
Nate's Destiny, Book Six
Blaine's Wager, Book Seven
Fletcher's Pride, Book Eight
Bay's Desire, Book Nine
Cam's Hope, Book Ten

Romantic Suspense

Eternal Brethren, Military Romantic Suspense

Steadfast, Book One
Shattered, Book Two
Haunted, Book Three
Untamed, Book Four
Devoted, Book Five
Faithful, Book Six, Coming Next in the Series!

Peregrine Bay, Romantic Suspense

Reclaiming Love, Book One
Our Kind of Love, Book Two
Edge of Love, Coming Next in the Series!

Contemporary Romance Series

MacLarens of Fire Mountain

Second Summer, Book One
Hard Landing, Book Two
One More Day, Book Three
All Your Nights, Book Four
Always Love You, Book Five
Hearts Don't Lie, Book Six
No Getting Over You, Book Seven
'Til the Sun Comes Up, Book Eight
Foolish Heart, Book Nine

Burnt River

Thorn's Journey
Del's Choice
Boone's Surrender

The best way to stay in touch is to subscribe to my newsletter. Go to www.shirleendavies.com and subscribe in the box at the top of the right column that asks for your email. You'll be notified of new books before they are released, have chances to win great prizes, and receive other subscriber-only specials.

Cam's Hope

MacLarens of Boundary Mountain Historical Western Romance Series

SHIRLEEN DAVIES

Book Ten in the MacLarens of Boundary Mountain

Historical Western Romance Series

Avalanche Ranch Press, LLC
PO Box 12618
Prescott, AZ 86304

Book design and conversions by Joseph Murray at 3rdplanetpublishing.com

Cover design by Kim Killion, The Killion Group

ISBN: 978-1-947680-11-1

I care about quality, so if you find something in error, please contact me via email at shirleen@shirleendavies.com

Description

A fierce, protective rancher.
A woman on the run from her father's shadowy past.

Cam's Hope, Book Ten, MacLarens of Boundary Mountain Historical Western Romance Series

Camden MacLaren is a rancher to his core, working long hours to continue the success of the family's ranch, Circle M. Although a cattleman, his expertise is in training horses, breeding and preparing them to fulfill Army contracts. Yet, he yearned for something more—the love of a woman strong enough for the hard life as a rancher's wife.

Evangeline Rousseau made one adventurous decision in her life. After her parents' deaths, she'd packed her belongings and moved across country to settle in the frontier town where her best friend lived. Buying her own house and settling in, she found herself wondering how a city girl such as herself could find a future in a town of ranchers, men who made a living with their hands.

The attraction between them was immediate, yet Cam hesitated to express his increasing desire for a woman with no knowledge of cattle, horses, or making a living from the land. No matter the intense pull between them, a beautiful, sheltered woman such as Vangie would find little happiness away from the advantages of a town.

Cam's reasons to keep his distance fall away when threats are directed at Vangie. Men from her father's past are hunting her down, following a trail from Grand Rapids to Conviction. The reason for their search is simple. Collect money Vangie's father allegedly owed them, and they'll use any means necessary to get it.

Cam's Hope, book ten in the MacLarens of Boundary Mountain Historical Western Romance Series, is a stand-alone, full-length novel with an HEA and no cliffhanger.

Visit my website for a list of characters for each series.

http://www.shirleendavies.com/character-list.html

Cam's Hope

Prologue

Conviction, Northern California
June 1867

Camden MacLaren sat with his family near the front of the church, his attention locked on the maid of honor. Evangeline Rousseau stood by her childhood friend and beautiful bride, Suzette Gasnier. After several painful years, she and Bayard Donahue would be joined in marriage a second time.

Doing her best to appear discreet, Vangie shot a quick look over her shoulder at the second row, tensing when her gaze locked on Cam's. She'd been caught. Worse, she couldn't miss his smug expression at her obvious interest.

Vangie pursed her lips, vowing to do a better job of concealing her attraction. From what Suzette had told her, the handsome rancher had no problem drawing female attention.

The reverend introducing Mr. and Mrs. Donahue to the guests pulled her from thoughts of Cam in time to watch Bay take advantage of the moment, bending Suzette over his arm for a searing kiss. The action caused the crowd to applaud and cheer, sealing the joy everyone felt.

Following the couple out of the church, Vangie couldn't help taking one more glance at Cam. He no longer watched her, his focus on the people around him.

The MacLarens were a large family with a sprawling, prosperous ranch east of town. She'd heard they also had vast amounts of land north of Conviction, near Settlers Valley. A city girl, her interest came more from curiosity than any understanding of the wealth inherent in the land.

Stepping outside, Bay shook hands while Suzette was engulfed by several women before leading them to the Feather River Restaurant.

Within minutes, all chairs were occupied, servers moving from one table to the next, filling glasses with champagne. Vangie couldn't keep the smile from her face at the genuine love so many people had for Bay and Suzette. For the first time since her parents died, she truly felt as if she belonged.

Taking a seat at the table with the newlyweds, she relaxed, enjoying the easy banter between the guests. A hearty laugh drew her attention to a group of men. Several MacLarens stood with Griff MacKenzie, a good friend of Bay and Suzette's. In the middle stood Cam, his head tilted back in laughter. She saw the instant he spotted her.

One moment he was ten feet away. The next, he stood beside her. "Is this chair taken?"

Lips parting, she stared up at him. "Um, no...I don't believe so."

"Good."

He'd barely sat down when Griff took the seat on the opposite side of her.

"Quite the wedding." Holding up his glass, he tilted it toward Bay and Suzette. "To my closest friends. Remember this day and don't make the same mistakes."

Raising her glass, Vangie took a sip, understanding Griff's meaning. No matter their problems, her friends had found their way back to each other.

"You seem to be settling in here, lass. Do you plan to stay?"

Vangie's gaze met Cam's, her stomach churning at how close he sat. They'd spent some time together when Suzette had been taken by outlaws. At the time, Cam had been recovering from a gunshot wound and couldn't ride with the men searching for her. Sitting erect, his broad shoulders taking up more than his share of space, he no longer showed signs of ever being hurt.

"I do like it here. Whether I'll stay or not..." Vangie looked at Suzette. With her marriage, Vangie no longer felt comfortable staying in Bay's home. "I'm still deciding."

"If you don't mind me giving my thoughts, lass, I'd like to see you stay."

Straightening, her attention shifted to the entrance when the front door burst open. A man dressed in dusty black pants, coat, and well-worn hat stood there. Above average in height, his shoulders were broad, thick arms straining the fabric of his coat. Her audible gasp caught Cam's attention.

"Do you know him, Vangie?" Cam asked as the man took several steps inside.

Eyes wide, she didn't answer before Cam, Bay, and Griff stood, walking toward the man at the same time Brodie stopped in front of him.

"I'm Sheriff MacLaren. Are you here for Bay and Suzette?"

The man shot Brodie a cursory glance, not answering before searching the faces in the room.

Brodie tried again. "I'm sorry, lad. The restaurant is closed for a wedding celebration."

Not finding who he sought, the man looked back at him for an instant. Turning toward the crowd, he opened his mouth, his loud, raspy voice vibrating throughout the room.

"I've come for Evangeline Rousseau, and I won't be leaving without her."

Chapter One

Circle M Ranch
A few days later...

"Move them toward the river, lad. Aye, that's the way." Cam swiped a sleeve over his damp forehead, not taking his gaze off his younger cousin, Thane. At sixteen, he'd been working the cattle for several years. Lately, Thane had been pestering his oldest brother, Quinn, for more responsibility.

Today's short cattle drive, moving the animals from one pasture to another, was one more test of Thane's ability. Even with the smaller herd, the change would normally require at least three men. Today, it was just the two of them, and the young man had done a remarkable job. Serious and focused on the task, Thane held qualities of both his older brothers, Quinn and Bram. If the decision were up to Cam, Thane would already be on his way north to work with Blaine.

He understood firsthand how it felt to be under the constant scrutiny of two older brothers. Cam couldn't fault Colin or Blaine for being somewhat overprotective of their younger siblings. Losing their father a short time after reaching Conviction forced the older children to grow up fast, guard those they loved.

Kicking Duke, his golden palomino gelding, Cam rode forward from his position on the left, keeping a few head from straying into the dense brush. Thane did the same on the right, then pulled back to the drag position to keep the animals moving forward.

It didn't take long to reach the pasture and settle the herd. Thane would bunk down with the cattle that night, but Cam wouldn't be with him.

After staying away from town a few days, letting his cousin, Brodie, deal with the surprise appearance of a man from Vangie's past, Cam decided it was time he got some answers for himself.

Since the wedding, Brodie hadn't ridden out to Circle M. Which meant Cam knew nothing more than what he'd witnessed in the restaurant. Bay and Griff had escorted Suzette and Vangie from the building while his brother questioned the man.

He'd felt less than useless when Vangie's face widened in surprise. She knew the man. How well, Cam didn't know, but he meant to find out.

Leaving Thane to take care of the herd, he took a circuitous route to the MacLaren ranch, composed of several houses and barns surrounded by numerous corrals. It had taken years to become the prosperous ranch they'd dreamed of when escaping Scotland for a better life.

Their short time farming outside of Philadelphia had been less than successful. The promise of a better future had come from learning about a large piece of land available in northern California.

It had been a huge risk for the struggling MacLaren clan. As always, they'd pooled their savings, purchased the land and four Conestoga wagons before joining a group traveling west.

The small nugget of hope had been carefully cultivated. Within a few years, Circle M had become a name recognized throughout the state. The oldest cousins had married, as had a couple of their younger brothers and sisters. With each new union, Cam experienced a jolt of loss, a feeling of being left behind.

He'd never thought much about marriage or children, figuring someday, he'd meet the right woman and bring her into the family. Meeting Vangie had brought someday to the present. Every minute he'd spent with her strengthened his resolve to learn more about the intriguing woman. The man showing up at the restaurant had stalled his plans, not stopped them. If he had to fight ten suitors for the right to court Vangie, he would.

Conviction

"I don't understand why you came all this way to find me, Eustice. Leaving Grand Rapids was what I wanted." Vangie kept her words simple so her longtime friend would understand.

They'd met in the schoolhouse when both were children. He'd been a couple years older. Much bigger than the other boys, his size belied a gentle, protective nature. He was also one of the smartest children in the overcrowded classroom.

More than once, the unassuming Eustice Hadley had come to the aid of those smaller, least able to defend themselves from the few, yet persistent bullies. He'd done it more than once for Vangie. So it came as a blow to her and most of the children when they learned Eustice had been involved in an accident which rendered him unable to communicate past a ten-year-old level.

Throughout the years, they'd stayed close. Then her parents had died and she'd made the difficult decision to head west. It had been Eustice who'd seen her off, tears welling in both their eyes at her departure. Now he sat in the parlor of Bay and Suzette's home, and he was scared.

"Why did you come all this way, Eustice?"

Nervously picking at a spot on his trousers, he rocked back and forth, rubbing a hand over his face. "I told the sheriff, Vangie. I told him over and over, but he doesn't believe me."

"Told him what, Eustice?"

Continuing to rock in the large, overstuffed chair, his gaze shot to Bay and Suzette across the room. "The men who want to find you."

"Men?"

"Two men. They wanted to know how to find you." He stopped rocking, clasping his hands together. "I promise I didn't tell them, Vangie. But they came back. One time they pointed a gun at me, but I still didn't tell them. They are very bad men."

Reaching out, she placed a comforting hand on his arm, her voice gentle. "I'm sorry they scared you."

"They didn't scare me, Vangie." His gaze darted around the room before meeting hers. "I was mad because they wanted to find you and I knew they were bad."

Bay moved to sit next to Eustice. "Do you know if they followed you to Conviction?"

Giving several quick shakes of his head, Eustice stared down at his hands. "I don't know."

Squeezing his arm, Vangie leaned forward, forcing him to look at her. "It's all right. You came to warn me. Eustice, this is important. Do you know their names?"

Shaking his head again, he lowered his face into his hands. "No."

"Would you be able to recognize them if they come to Conviction?" Bay asked.

Lifting his head, Eustice nodded. "Yes."

"That's wonderful." Vangie settled her small, slender hand over his large, calloused one. "Now, is someone taking care of your blacksmith shop?"

Rocking again, he pulled his hand away, clasping it in his lap. "I sold it to come here."

"Sold it? But you loved your work."

"I needed to tell you about the men, Vangie. Don't be angry with me."

"I'm not angry with you, Eustice. It's just, well..." She expelled a slow breath. "I know how much you liked having your own shop."

His eyes lit up, a question in them. "I can be a blacksmith here. Isn't that right, Mr. Donahue?"

Leaning forward, the corners of Bay's mouth tilted up. "I'll see what I can find out about a job. And remember, Eustice, I asked you to call me Bay."

Brows furrowing, mouth drawing into a tight line, he nodded. "All right."

"Good. For today, you stay here with Suzette and Vangie while I see about a blacksmith job for you."

"I should come with you."

"Not today, Eustice. It would be best if you stayed here. There is one man I need to talk with. If all goes well, I'll be back with good news."

Resting his hands on the arms of the sturdy chair, he shoved himself up. "Thank you, Mr....I mean, Bay." Holding out his hand, Eustice offered one of his rare smiles when Bay clasped it.

A rap on the front door had Bay striding the short distance to open it. "Cam. Please, come inside and I'll introduce you to Eustice."

Stepping across the threshold, he removed his hat, fingering the brim as he moved into the parlor. "Good evening, Suzette, Vangie." His attention then moved to the tall, broad-shouldered man who stepped a little in front of Vangie in a protective gesture.

"Cam, this is Eustice Hadley. He's a friend of Vangie's from Grand Rapids. Eustice, this is Camden MacLaren."

Cam's hand wasn't small, but when he offered it to Eustice, the big man's hand engulfed his. "A pleasure, Mr. Hadley."

"Eustice," he muttered, drawing his hand away.

The hesitation and timid actions prompted Cam to study the physically imposing man. Today, he didn't show the intimidating presence he did at the restaurant. Glancing at Vangie, he didn't miss the almost imperceptible shake of her head, as if she understood his thoughts.

"Eustice and I grew up together, Cam. He owned a blacksmith shop before coming west to find me."

"I came for Vangie before those men find her."

"Men?" Cam asked.

"Eustice told us about two men in Grand Rapids who've been searching for me. They're the reason he sold his blacksmith shop and came west."

"To protect Vangie." Eustice's big hands rubbed up and down his thighs. "They're very bad men."

"Why do you have to protect her, lad? Surely they wouldn't travel all the way to Conviction."

Lifting his face, the lines around his eyes deepening, Eustice shook his head at Cam. "I think they will come here. They want Vangie, but they can't have her."

Jaw clenching, Cam leaned forward, making certain he had Eustice's attention. "Did the men ever tell you why they wanted to find Vangie?"

Shoulders stiffening, he glanced at her before nodding. "Yes."

"What was their reason, lad?" Cam asked.

Throat working, his breath came in short gasps as his focus moved to Vangie. "They're looking for the money."

"What are your thoughts on Eustice?" Cam walked alongside Bay on the way to Conviction's only blacksmith shop.

"If he believes there's a danger to Vangie, I'm inclined to agree." Bay repeated the man's story, the same as Vangie told it to him and Suzette. "According to her, Eustice isn't capable of lying. Remember, he sold his blacksmith shop to afford the trip west. A shop Vangie says he loved more than anything."

"Except Vangie," Cam muttered.

"Yes, he does love her. The same as you love your sisters and cousins. He's been protective of Vangie since she was eight. Not even the accident changed his bond with her. Which means, I don't see Eustice leaving Conviction anytime soon. That's why we're going to speak with Mr. Jones."

"It would be the perfect solution for the lad."

"And the town. Jones told me a couple weeks ago if he didn't find a buyer, he'd be closing up within ninety days. That would leave a good number of people without livery and blacksmith services."

"Aye, it would. If Jones and Eustice don't reach an agreement, maybe it's time we open a second shop."

Slipping between passing wagons and riders, the two crossed the deeply rutted street. "*We?*"

"Aye, lad. My uncles will talk to August, who'll include you and Griff as partners." His mouth curved upward at Bay's resigned expression. August Fielder had brought Bay, then Griff into his esteemed law firm. Over the years, August and the MacLarens had participated in several profitable partnerships. "Now, it may not come to that, lad. Not if you convince Jones to sell to Eustice."

Pursing his lips, Bay shot a withering glance at Cam. "Then I'd best get this settled right away."

Chapter Two

Grand Rapids

"We never should've believed Hadley when he said Evangeline left for Chicago to visit relatives. The man may be slow, but he isn't stupid. We pushed too hard, and he lied to us." Merle Riordan leaned toward his older brother, Reginald, lowering his voice. "Now Hadley *and* the woman are gone."

"We'll find her."

"She could be anywhere, Reg."

Leaning back, he waited as the server refilled their cups with the worst coffee he'd ever tasted. "I don't know why we came here. The food is barely passable, and the coffee is worse." Still, he picked up the cup, grimacing as the tepid liquid rolled down his throat.

"It's quite simple. Nobody we know would consider coming here for a meal."

Gaze moving over Reg's tailored suit and black Congress shoes he'd ordered from Europe, Merle had to agree. Dressed in a similar fashion, his eyes crinkled in amusement at the idea one of their sophisticated, college-bred chums might enter such an establishment.

Chipped paint, browned from years of unending cigar and cigarette smoke, was the best quality of the small café. Marred wood tables, rickety chairs at least forty years old, and a floor so uneven Merle wondered how often the servers tripped, slamming plates onto patrons' laps. The idea had him stifling a chuckle.

"What's so amusing?"

Features sobering, Merle crossed his arms, gaze flitting between the patrons inside and the rain flooding the street. "Nothing about any of this is amusing, Reg. We've already lost too much time trying to locate a woman who has nothing more than the proceeds from the sale of her family home. Not nearly enough to repay the loan we made to her father. For all we know, she's already spent every cent."

Tapping the table with three fingers, Reginald appeared to study one of the many gouges in the tabletop. "There was more."

"Impossible. Her father came to us out of desperation." Merle again lowered his voice. "*Financial* desperation."

"That doesn't mean his wife didn't have jewelry he wouldn't have dared touch. There was also a life insurance policy taken out a month before the accident which killed him and his wife."

Eyes widening, Merle's face took on a red tinge. "You never mentioned anything about insurance. How much?"

"More than enough to repay the loan."

"And Evangeline was the sole beneficiary?"

"Yes. So you see, the young woman would have more than enough to live quite comfortably for a long time. We just need to find her."

Quiet settled over the table while the middle-aged woman placed full plates in front of them. "Anything else?"

"No, this will be all." Placing a bite of eggs into his mouth, Merle's face contorted at the foul taste of stale lard. "We truly must find another spot to meet. There has to be a place beyond the eyes of our acquaintances with decent food."

Swallowing the burnt toast with a swallow of coffee, Reginald set down his fork. "We won't be needing to meet here any longer."

"Well, we can't meet at our homes. Not with wives too curious for their own good."

Shoving his plate aside, Reginald swept crumbs from his jacket, grimacing at a small stain on the front of his shirt. "We won't need a new location as we'll be leaving to find Miss Rousseau."

Choking on the last of his coffee, Merle shot a look at the woman behind the counter, assured she stood out of earshot. "How can we follow her if we have no idea where she may have gone?"

"All we have to do is follow Eustice Hadley. I've discovered he took the train a day after the last time we spoke with him. Fortunately for us, he's quite memorable. Large frame, worn clothing, accommodating manner, slow of speech. The clerk at the rail office recalled him quite well."

"Did you learn where he went?" Merle asked.

"The clerk recalled Eustice saying he planned to travel to California."

Circle M

"Can you believe the lad, Cam?" Colin groomed his stallion, Chieftain, talking to him in whispers while continuing his conversation with his youngest brother.

"Vangie believes him. So do Bay and Suzette." Leaning against the stall, Cam crossed his arms.

"Aye, but do *you* think men are looking for the lass?"

Staring up at the barn loft, Cam thought of Eustice's face when he talked of the men, the anger in his voice. "Aye, I do."

"Did you talk to Brodie?"

"Nae. Bay wanted to wait until he talked with August and Griff."

"The lad will be living at the livery, same as Mr. Jones?" Colin tossed the brush into a pail before leading Chieftain to the pasture behind the barn. "I'd be guessing there's no other place to stay."

Shoving away from the stall, Cam grabbed the bucket, placing it on a shelf. "Eustice will be living with Bay and Suzette for a while."

"Ach, now that will be interesting. Didn't you say the lad is in love with Vangie?"

"*Protective* of her. Maybe a wee bit more than needed. They've known each other since she was a lassie. Eustice is two years older."

Chuckling, Colin strode toward a pile of frayed rope. Picking one up, he studied the damage. "Will you be courting the lass?"

"Courting?"

"Aye, lad. Deciding if there might be a future with her."

Shaking his head, Cam grabbed one of the remaining lengths of rope. "Nae. I like the lass, nothing more."

"Ach, here you are." Quinn walked toward them, stopping next to Cam. "You left for town yesterday before telling me your thoughts on Thane. How did the lad do?"

"He's better than any of us at his age. You should be sending the lad to work with Blaine."

Colin's eyes widened, but he held his tongue. Quinn didn't.

"Nae. Thane's needed here. We can't be sending him north."

"Blaine's short of good men, and it would be good for Thane to get away from here."

Crossing his arms, Quinn shot a cold glare at Cam. "You're meaning away from *me*."

"Nae. It's time the lad had a chance without older brothers and cousins watching his every move. He's no cousins his age, no one to talk to the way the rest of the lads had."

"He'll have it no better with Blaine," Quinn said.

"Aye, he will. You asked my opinion, and I've given it to you." Tossing the rope back on the pile, Cam left, heading outside.

"Wait." Quinn jogged toward him. "You're sure about this?"

"Aye. He's a better rancher at sixteen than any of us were. If the lad stays here, he'll be waiting longer for the responsibility he's earned. Blaine will give it to him right away."

Hands on hips, Quinn's gaze moved across the expanse of houses and barns. It had taken years of hard work, failings, and successes to build Circle M into the largest ranch north of Sacramento. Though young, Thane had worked alongside the older men and women, doing as much or more work than the others. Their late father, Gillis, would be proud of his youngest son.

"Colin let Blaine go, Quinn. Maybe it's time for you to do the same with Thane."

Continuing to stare into the distance, he slowly turned toward Cam. "Aye, you may be right. Ma won't be happy about sending the lad away."

Clasping Quinn's shoulder, he shook his head. "Nae, she won't."

"Eustice is already doing quite the business, Vangie." Bay poured himself another cup of coffee, holding up the pot. "Would you care for more?"

"No, this is fine. He does seem quite happy and much more at ease. I think he just needed to start working again. Eustice has never been comfortable sitting around. He needs to be productive."

"If the last few days are an indication, he has enough work for a couple weeks, and the livery is full." Taking a seat behind his desk in the law office, Bay set down the cup. "Now, tell me why you need legal advice."

Reaching into her reticule, she withdrew a piece of paper, sliding it across the desk. "I need your opinion on how to protect my savings."

Not expecting much, Bay picked up the paper, his brows lifting. "This is quite a sum, Vangie. Is it all from the sale of your family home?"

Straightening, she leaned forward. "The house, life insurance on both my parents, and a savings account. I plan to buy a house in town, but beyond that, I'm unsure of what to do." Letting out a shaky breath, she pursed her lips. "I'm concerned Eustice is right and there are men after me for the money. As you can see, the funds are all in the Bank of Conviction."

"There isn't a better managed bank in town, Vangie. August Fielder is the main shareholder, and the MacLarens own a large stake."

"I'm more concerned about having all the funds in one place. What if there's a robbery? I'd end up with nothing, Bay. I wondered if it might be best to divide the money between two banks."

"The San Francisco Merchant Bank is the only other choice. It's had a rough start, but is gaining more customers each month. Mostly people new to Conviction who know little of the town history." Placing his cup down, he walked to the window, peering out onto the crowded street below. "If it would make you feel safer, you can certainly move some of the money over."

Chewing her lower lip, Vangie understood Bay's thoughts on the two banks. His employer and mentor, August Fielder, had played a large part in the Bank of Conviction's success.

"I won't do anything right away. I would appreciate your help locating a house, though."

Still staring onto the street, he abruptly turned, holding up a finger. "Stay here."

Without waiting for her response, he grabbed his gunbelt, strapping it on as he rushed down the stairs.

"Mr. Donahue?" Jasper Hamm, the office secretary called after him, but Bay didn't stop.

Shoving open the door, the sound of gunfire had him drawing his gun, crouching down.

Sheriff Brodie MacLaren stood on the other side of the street next to Sam Covington, one of his deputies and his brother-in-law. On Bay's side of the street were two more deputies, Seth Montero and Alex Campbell. All four had their guns aimed at three men, their backs to each other, six-shooters drawn.

"Drop your guns, lads, or you won't be leaving town alive." Brodie took a step closer, spotting Bay on the other side of the street. Giving a quick shake of his head to warn off his friend, Brodie's mouth twisted when Bay continued to aim his six-shooter at the three men.

Sam moved farther away from Brodie, forcing the outlaws to divide their attention further. "You didn't get what you came for. Why die when you can spend a few years behind bars and go free?"

Inching away from the cover of a bench outside his office, Bay didn't take his focus off the men. He had no plans to shoot unless the three opened fire. Even then, between Brodie and his deputies, it was doubtful the outlaws would be alive within seconds of the first shot.

Releasing a relieved breath, he lowered his weapon when the three dropped their guns, raising their hands. Seconds later, a shot from behind Bay took down one of the outlaws.

Whipping around, he spotted a lone rider, a rifle in one hand. Raising the gun, Bay fired two shots, missing when the horse danced around. Reining south, he kicked the animal, racing away from town.

"Get a doctor." Seth knelt by the wounded man, Alex standing next to him with his aim on the other two outlaws while Brodie and Sam raced to Eustice's livery for their own mounts.

Running to help, Bay dropped down beside Seth. Seeing the man's eyes glazed and fixed, he shifted toward the deputy. "He's gone."

"What happened?"

Both looked up to see Doc Vickery running toward them, a black satchel in his hand. Before he reached them, Bay held up a hand.

"He's dead, Doc."

Standing, Seth and Alex escorted the other two outlaws to the jail while Vickery checked the man's pulse and breathing. Leaning back on his haunches, he shook his head.

"The bullet hit an artery in his thigh. I couldn't have saved the man even if I'd been standing right beside him." Glancing around, Vickery's brows drew together. "Who did this?"

Shaking his head, Bay straightened, holstering his gun. "A lone rider with a rifle. He took off south when I fired at him."

Staring past Bay to the road out of Conviction, Vickery rubbed his jaw. "I wonder why he'd shoot one man out of the three and ride off. It doesn't make sense to me. Were they armed?"

Following the doctor's gaze, Bay gave a slow shake of his head. "They'd just dropped their guns when he fired."

Vickery was right. Something was very wrong. He just hoped Brodie found the killer before he returned to take care of the other two men.

Chapter Three

"We lost him a couple miles down the trail to Sacramento. Never got close enough to get a good look." Voice full of disgust, Sam tossed his hat on the desk in the jail. "Could you identify him if he comes back, Bay?"

"It's doubtful. I locked on his rifle and fired. Nothing else caught my attention." Lowering himself into a chair, Bay massaged the back of his neck. "Except the clothes were different than what you usually see around here."

"What do you mean, lad?" Brodie brushed dust from his shirt, making no apology as it settled on his desk and floor.

"His hat was dark, maybe black. One of those French beret types. I've seen the Basque sheepherders wear something similar. I also remember a long coat, also black. Much too big for the rider." Bay stretched his legs out, crossing them at the ankles.

"Beard or mustache?" Sam asked.

"I couldn't tell from my position. He was aiming to shoot again when I fired and he took off." Bay's mouth twisted into a grim line. "I can't believe I missed him."

"You did fine, lad. Scaring him away may have saved more lives." Brodie set his hat on a hook and sat down. "Seth and Alex are talking to the townsfolk. Maybe someone will remember him."

"He's not from here, Brodie." Rubbing his jaw, Bay glanced behind him at the window. "What were those three men doing?"

"Tried to rob the bank."

Bay shifted back to look at Sam. "August's bank?"

"Aye," Brodie answered. "It was wise of him to add another lad for security. The two guards spotted the robbers the instant they walked inside."

Standing, Bay motioned toward the cells in the back. "Do you mind if I take a look at the prisoners?"

"Nae, but I'll be coming with you."

Following Brodie, Bay moved to just outside the bars, studying their clothing. "The coats are similar, but the hats are different. Theirs are flat with floppy brims."

Brodie jangled the keys to get the men's attention. "Did you recognize the shooter, lads?"

One of the men flashed him a nervous look, his jaw twitching, but he didn't speak. The other stared at the floor, shaking his head.

"Are you certain? He killed one of your lads. Don't you want us to find him?"

When neither answered, Brodie scrubbed a hand down his face. "If we find him, I'm thinking I'll be putting him in the same cell as you two."

Both stiffened, although neither spoke.

Stepping next to Brodie, Bay wrapped his fingers around the bars. "He was ready to shoot again when I fired at him. If he hadn't been scared off, one of you would be at the undertaker's right now. I'm certain you know who he is and why he came after you. There's a better chance the sheriff and his deputies can protect you if they have an idea of who wants you dead."

The man staring at the floor rose, hands fisted at his sides. "Jean-Paul will get to us anyway. He's been ordered to kill us, and he never disappoints."

"Jean-Paul?" Brodie asked.

Looking away, he sat back down. "I've said enough."

Motioning for Bay to follow, Brodie walked to the front, noting Seth and Alex had returned. "Have any of you lads heard of a man named Jean-Paul?"

"I haven't," Sam answered. "Why?"

"One of the prisoners called the shooter by that name, but wouldn't say anything more."

Bay rested a hip against Brodie's desk. "Except that he was ordered to kill them. He also implied Jean-Paul always completes his orders."

"I'll send a telegram to Pinkerton. Maybe Allan has heard of him and can provide a last name. He might even have a sketch of him in the files."

"It's a good idea, Sam." Brodie stared out the front window. "We know he wears a black beret and coat, and carries a rifle. Keep watch for him, lads.

27

There's no doubt Jean-Paul will return to finish the job."

"It was all quite frightening." Vangie refilled Suzette's cup with tea. "I watched from the window in Bay's office. The men had dropped their guns. An instant later, I heard a shot and one of the men fell to the ground. I'm certain he was dead."

"It must've been hard seeing a man shot. Are you all right, Vangie?" Suzette understood how it felt, having seen men killed after being kidnapped a couple months before. Several men died when Bay, Brodie, and a few others came to rescue her. Seeing the blood and vacant eyes had been terrifying.

"Yes, it was. I hope to never witness anything like it again."

"You aren't considering leaving Conviction, are you, Vangie?"

Eyes widening, she shook her head. "Not at all. People were murdered in Grand Rapids. It's just I was never there to see it. Killings can happen anywhere."

The sound of the front door opening and closing had them turning toward the entry. Standing, Suzette wrapped her arms around Bay's waist. Hugging her, he spotted Vangie in the parlor.

"Sorry you had to witness what happened." Dropping his arms, he moved past Suzette to Vangie, taking her hands in his. "Are you all right?"

A short burst of laughter escaped. "Suzette asked the same. I'm fine, Bay, although I hope to never witness a murder again."

"What were the outlaws after?"

Placing an arm around his wife's waist, he stroked a finger down her cheek. "They tried to rob the Bank of Conviction. Thankfully, August had hired a second guard. They suspected the three men the instant they entered the bank. Sam was the only customer at the time. The robbers separated, one going to the window, demanding money. Sam and the two guards drew their guns at the same time. One of the guards ran to the jail to get Brodie. When Sam escorted them outside, the men drew their own weapons, standing back to back in the middle of the street." He looked at Vangie. "You witnessed the rest."

"Do you know who killed one of the men?" Suzette asked.

"Only that he goes by Jean-Paul, which isn't much. Sam's contacting Pinkerton."

"A gypsy?" Vangie asked.

Bay's brow lifted. "What do you mean?"

"Well, I only got a glimpse of him, but the hat he wore, as well as the name, indicate he may be a Romani. A gypsy, as most call them."

Suzette cocked her head. "How would you know that, Vangie?"

"Father took me out to their camp outside Grand Rapids a few times. He said he had some type of business to conduct. While he disappeared into a wagon, I stayed by their campfire, watching them sing and dance. They were always quite lively and fun. Most times, one of the young women would join me. That's where I learned a little about them. The person who shot the bank robber may not be Romani, but the hat and name indicate the possibility."

Bay rubbed a finger over his brow. "I haven't heard of a gypsy camp near Conviction."

"Neither have I, and I hear all kinds of things at the restaurant. I'll ask Zeke. He often takes long rides when he's not working." Suzette mentioned her assistant manager, a man who hadn't been in Conviction long. He'd turned out to be one of her best employees.

"I'll let Brodie know Vangie's thoughts. He or one of his deputies may have noticed a settlement in the area."

A knock on the door drew Bay's attention. Opening it, a knowing smile broke across his face. "Cam. Please, come in."

"If I'm not intruding." He didn't wait for a response before stepping inside.

"Not at all. What brings you to town?"

"Supplies. I stopped at the jail and Brodie told me what happened." Removing his hat, he looked at Vangie. "My brother said you saw it happen."

"I did, and please don't ask me if I'm all right, because I am."

A slow smile spread across his face. "Aye, lass, I can see that."

Vangie's eyes flashed, lips parting, but she didn't reply.

Bay nodded at her. "Vangie thinks the man who killed the bank robber might be connected to traveling gypsies."

"And why would you be thinking that?" Cam asked.

Shrugging, she stood, picking up the teapot. "His clothing and name." Walking into the kitchen, she glanced over her shoulder, seeing Cam following her.

"Brodie said one of the prisoners said his name is Jean-Paul. Is that a name associated with gypsies?"

Setting the pot down, she began to prepare more tea. "It can be. Plus, he wore a hat I've seen gypsy men wear. A beret some French or Basque males wear. My suggestion may be completely wrong, but I wanted to tell Bay in case there is a connection. He mentioned not seeing one of their camps in the area. Suzette is going to ask Zeke if he's seen them on his rides, and Bay's going to speak with Brodie."

"There's no need for that, lass."

Wiping her hands on a towel, she turned toward him. "And why is that?"

"Because there *is* an encampment between town and Circle M."

"Really?" Excitement crept into her voice.

"Aye, lass. They are well off the trail, but we know where they are. My cousin, Thane, rode close enough to see them. He told a wild story of loud music, dancing, women wearing odd head ornaments and swirling skirts. And..." Cam glanced away, deciding not to continue.

"And what?"

"It's not important, lass."

"Oh no. You are not going to tease me, Camden MacLaren. What else did your cousin see?"

Scratching his head, he grimaced. This wasn't a conversation he wanted to have with any woman, and definitely not Vangie.

Taking a step closer, a glint of amusement sparkled in her eyes. "Tell me."

Although he knew her low, sultry voice was in jest, he took a step back. "Uh..."

Touching his arm, she chuckled. "Do you know your face turns red when you're uneasy?"

Crossing his arms, Cam glared at her. "Nae, I'm not uneasy."

"Yes, you are. The instant my voice changed, you stiffened. Which is good."

Blinking, he gave her a blank stare. "Good?"

"Very good. You see, I'm practicing."

Brows knitting together, his lips drew into a hard line. "Practicing for what?"

"To fulfill my dream of being an actress." Without another word, she whirled around, finishing the tea preparations.

Moving next to her, Cam leaned down. "You're teasing me, aren't you, lass?"

Placing the pot and cups on a tray, she lifted it for Cam to take, smiling up at him. "I might be."

Throwing back his head, he laughed. "You are the most confusing lass I've ever met, Vangie."

"Good."

Grinning, she strolled from the kitchen, leaving Cam holding the tray with his mouth gaping open.

Chapter Four

Cam crossed his arms, his hard expression unwavering. "You are not going with us, Vangie."

Glaring back, she settled fisted hands on her waist. "I certainly am, and there's nothing you can do to stop me."

Bay stood a few feet away, watching a friendly discussion shift to a heated exchange. After returning to the parlor, Cam had told Bay about the gypsy camp not far from the ranch. The men had immediately agreed to ride out to confirm their location before speaking with Brodie, a move both agreed would anger the sheriff. Still, they wanted to make certain the camp was still there before sending him and his deputies on a wild goose chase.

"Do you have a horse?" Cam asked.

"Well, no."

"You can use mine." Suzette ignored the scowls from Cam and Bay. "Eustice might even have one if mine isn't suitable for you."

"Yours will be fine, Suzette." She looked back at Cam. "Now that I have a horse, when do we leave?"

Sending a warning look at his wife, Bay's features softened. "It isn't wise for you to go with us. We don't know anything about these people, and it's quite possible the man who killed the outlaw is one of them.

It would be better if Cam and I go and let Brodie know what we find."

"I've been to their camps when they traveled through Michigan. Maybe I can help you talk to them about what happened."

"Cam and I can do that, Vangie."

"But they won't give you answers. At least none you'd be able to understand."

"What do you mean, lass?"

Clasping her hands together, she worried her bottom lip. "They are untrusting of outsiders. Even if they're certain one of theirs committed murder, they'd never give him up."

"Would they punish him?" Cam asked.

"Only if he committed a crime against his family, which is everyone in their camp. They see themselves as one large..." She glanced at Cam, a glint in her eyes. "A large clan, such as the MacLarens. They close up to protect their own."

"Ach, lass. You have my family wrong. We might do what we can to protect ours, but we wouldn't ignore the law. It's the reason Brodie is a good sheriff."

Vangie flushed at the intensity in his words. "I stand corrected. Gypsies are quite different in that respect. Instead of asking them if a Jean-Paul is part of their group, you must be much more subtle. In my opinion, it would be best to take Brodie with us now instead of waiting."

Cam shot a look at Bay. "Perhaps we should be including him and his deputies."

"No," Vangie interjected. "Not his deputies. It would be best if it's only the four of us."

"Lass..." Cam's voice trailed off when Vangie held up a hand.

"I'm going with you, so you might as well get used to the idea."

"She's right." Suzette moved next to Bay, placing her hand on his arm. "Vangie might be able to get information they wouldn't give to men."

"And Brodie shouldn't wear his badge. I doubt they'll talk to us at all if they suspect he's the sheriff. I'd best change clothes." Vangie headed up the stairs to her bedroom.

"All four of you should go, Bay. You and Vangie got a decent look at the man and might be able to spot him. As the sheriff, Brodie should ride along, and Cam knows where their camp is located."

Leaning down, Bay kissed her cheek. "And you?"

"Working at the restaurant, of course."

Omaha, Nebraska

"The driver recognized Hadley's description. He's certain he was on the stage west several weeks ago." Reggie tossed back the rest of the whiskey, a satisfied

36

smirk on his face. "Told you the blacksmith is too memorable for people to forget."

Merle rolled the glass between his fingers, watching as the amber liquid coated the sides. "Did you learn where Eustice was headed?"

"The stage went as far as Denver before heading back to Omaha. The driver didn't know where he went from there."

"At some point, there's a good chance we'll lose him and have no idea where to go next." Lifting the glass to his lips, Merle took a sip.

"I never said this would be an easy journey." Leaning forward, Reggie glanced around before lowering his voice. "Do I need to remind you the amount of money at stake is a great deal? Enough for you to leave your wife and marry your mistress, Merle."

Features twisting, he finished the last of the whiskey, setting the glass on the table hard enough to draw attention. "How many times do I have to tell you I've no intention of leaving my wife? I love her. It's just..."

"She doesn't provide what you need."

Motioning the bartender for a refill, Merle stared at the empty glass. "No, she doesn't. But she's a good woman."

"So the other women are?"

"The same as they are for you, Reggie. A diversion, nothing more. Besides, I have the children to consider. They love their mother. A divorce would ruin everything I've worked so hard to achieve."

"So what you're saying is the money—*our* money—Evangeline has means nothing to you."

"Of course I want the money back. I'm not sure your idea of tracking Eustice is the right way to find her. We've no proof she's the reason he left Grand Rapids."

"Don't be ridiculous, Merle. From what we learned, the man's been protecting her since they were children. He purposely sent us to Chicago in an attempt to buy himself time. When we returned, Hadley had already sold his blacksmith shop and headed west. Everyone we spoke to believes he's following her. We find Eustice, we find Evangeline. And our money."

Trail to Circle M

"You're certain the camp is out this way, lad?" Brodie kept his gaze moving, glad the almost full moon provided enough light to see.

"Aye. Thane found their camp and gave details of their location. The lad was concerned they were camped too close to Circle M not to be watched." Cam shifted, seeing Vangie riding alongside Bay.

"Have Colin and Quinn been checking on the camp?"

"Quinn rode out with Thane a few days ago, and they were still there. The lads said their camp would be hard to miss. They keep several fires going at night." Cam stared ahead and to his right. "Up ahead through the trees."

They reined up, waiting for Vangie and Bay to stop next to them.

"Are those their fires?" Bay asked.

"Should be." Cam looked at Brodie. "How do you want to do this?"

Leaning forward, he rested his arms on the saddle horn, his gaze fixed on the light of the fires. "We ride in together. If they don't draw on us, we'll continue closer and dismount, keeping watch on the gypsies and their camp. There's a chance the lad we want will be with them." Straightening, he looked at the others. "If he's smart, the lad will disappear inside a wagon and stay out of sight until we leave."

"What should I do, Brodie?"

His features softened at Vangie's unsure voice. "Stay close to us, lass. If it seems safe, you and Cam approach those who seem friendly while Bay and I stay back."

"None of them will be friendly." Vangie offered a small smile. "The gypsies aren't a trusting people. The reason the ones near home were hospitable was because they did business with my father."

"What kind of business, lass?" Cam asked.

"He was a banker. I always assumed he may have been lending them money, but..."

"But?" Cam prompted.

"It's nothing. Besides, my father is gone, so his business with the gypsies is no longer important."

"Are you two ready?" Bay asked.

Cam nodded, his mind still on Vangie's comment about her father. Something about the way her brows scrunched in confusion indicated she had a reason for her concern.

"Aye, we're ready."

Leading them forward at a slow pace, Brodie didn't take his focus off the camp ahead. Several people moved around the largest fire. As they got closer, he could hear a violin, along with boisterous laughter.

Reining to a stop twenty yards away, they studied the camp, each one mesmerized by two women dancing around the edges of the flames. Clapping, they whirled around, broad smiles on their faces. Then everything came to a stop.

They'd been spotted.

Brodie kicked his horse forward a few more paces before stopping when one of the men fired a shotgun into the air.

"You need to leave." A slender man of average height, wearing well-worn pants and coat, walked toward them, flanked by several others. Each carried a shotgun pointed at the four riders.

"You aren't welcome here." An older man, dressed in a similar fashion, moved to within a couple yards of Brodie, who'd positioned himself in front of the others.

"We saw your fires and thought you'd be letting us warm ourselves."

"Not possible. You need to ride out. *Now.*" Motioning with the barrel of the gun, he glanced at the others for support.

Inching her horse forward, Vangie dismounted, approaching the slack-jawed man with an appreciative smile. "I'm Evangeline Rousseau." Holding out her hand, she said nothing more, letting out a relieved breath when the man accepted it.

"Belcher Grey."

"We saw your fire, Mr. Grey, and hoped you'd let us stop for a bit."

He gestured behind her. "Who are those men?"

"My friends." Vangie motioned for them to dismount and come forward. "This is Brodie, Bay, and Cam." She looked at Belcher. "This is Mr. Grey."

Shaking hands, they kept their gazes moving around the camp, hoping Grey and the others didn't notice their interest.

"We have little. If you want to warm by the fire for a few minutes, you can. Then you must leave." Grey signaled the others to stand aside.

Vangie offered a warm smile. "Thank you, Mr. Grey. We won't stay long." She began to stroll past him. "Is this your family?"

"Yes. All are Greys."

"My father did business with a family much like yours. Their name was Lovel. Have you heard of them?"

Studying her a moment, he shook his head. "No."

He motioned for a woman close to his age to come closer. As she approached, Vangie noticed the heavy makeup and deep creases around her eyes and mouth.

"This is my wife, Brittanie."

Gaze narrowed, the older woman took in Vangie's hair and clothes. "What do you want?"

"My friends and I saw the fire. Your husband said we could warm ourselves before moving on."

Brittanie shot a venomous look at Grey, her mouth pinched in disgust. "They can't stay."

"They won't be staying. Ten minutes and they'll be gone."

"They'd better be, or the younger men will drive them off." The hate in Brittanie's eyes stunned Vangie.

"We aren't here to cause trouble, Mrs. Grey. A few minutes, then we'll ride out."

"See that you do." Picking up her skirts, Brittanie stormed off, disappearing into one of the wagons.

"She's a hard woman with a soft heart," Belcher mumbled, although his jaw tightened. He glanced at

Brodie, Bay, and Cam, who stood at another fire several feet away. "Which one is the sheriff?"

Vangie stiffened at the unexpected question. "Sheriff?"

Removing his hat, Belcher scratched his head. "I believe he's the man who rode in first. The one standing on the opposite side of the others. Am I right?"

Drawing back her hands warming at the fire, she clasped them together. "Yes. He's also a friend, as are Bay and Cam." As always happened, a slight grin lifted the corners of her mouth when she spoke Cam's name. "He's not here as the sheriff, Mr. Grey. Brodie and Cam are cousins. They're part of the MacLaren family."

The hard glint returned to his dark eyes. After a moment, his uncompromising gaze had her squirming. "Do not bring them back. No good will come from them returning."

Chapter Five

Circle M

"You met them, Cam?" Quinn stopped brushing his horse, pushing his hat back on his head.

"Aye." He didn't quite know how to explain the distrust and hostility on their faces. "They aren't a friendly lot. After a few minutes, they urged us to leave with a warning not to return."

"Are they on MacLaren land?"

"Nae. About a quarter of a mile east of the ranch's southern border."

Crossing his arms, Quinn leaned against a stall. "Close enough to steal our cattle."

"Aye. Brodie said the same."

"What did the lad say?"

They turned at Colin's voice. He walked into the barn with Thane. Bram, Quinn and Thane's other brother, followed a moment later, rubbing his hands together.

"The new colt is going to be a grand part of our breeding program." Pulling a stool from a corner, Bram sat down, the joy on his face causing the others to smile.

"I've not seen you this excited about a colt in a long time, lad." Quinn grabbed another stool, setting it beside Bram.

"You must come see him. Cam and I've been working with all the other colts, but this one is going to be important, lads. The Circle M will be the finest horse breeding ranch in all of California."

"Aye, if the gypsies don't take them," Thane muttered.

"Gypsies?" Bram asked.

"We've a camp of them not far from our southern border," Quinn said. "Cam, Brodie, and Bay visited them last night."

Colin's brow lifted. "Aye?"

"Some lads tried to rob the bank yesterday. Brodie and his deputies got them to drop their guns right before a man rode in and shot one of them. Bay fired several shots and drove him away." Removing his hat, he shoved a hand through his hair. "Vangie saw the man, too. She thought his clothing similar to those worn by gypsies. That, and the killer's name."

"His name?" Colin asked.

"Aye. The two remaining robbers were taken to the jail. One of them said the shooter's name was Jean-Paul. Vangie says it's a common name among some gypsy families."

"So you rode out with Brodie and Bay," Quinn said.

"And Vangie. The lass was the one who got their leader, Belcher Grey, to let us stay a few minutes." Shaking his head, Cam chuckled. "I wanted the lass to stay behind. Turned out she was the only one they'd talk to."

"Was the shooter in the camp?" Thane asked.

"We didn't see the lad, but it doesn't mean he wasn't hiding in one of the wagons. It might be best if we move the colts and fillies to corrals at the north end of the compound, Bram."

"Aye. We don't want to be taking chances of them disappearing."

Cam followed Bram outside. "You know Colin and Quinn will devise a plan to guard the ranch and the horse stock."

Shoving both hands into his pockets, Bram walked toward the corral where the colts were kept. "Aye. It's a good thing. We've a good reputation for raising cattle, but the young horses are the ranch's future." Stepping onto the bottom rung of the fence, he rested his arms on top. "Will you be going to town tonight?"

Cam halted when he moved to step up beside Bram. "Why would I be going to town?"

Cocking a brow, his mouth twisted in amusement. "The lass you want is there, isn't she?"

"Vangie is a bonny one. It doesn't mean I've an interest in her."

"So now you've turned to lying?"

Lips thinning, Cam opened his mouth to respond, then closed it.

"I've seen the way you are with her. Don't be telling me you've no interest. The question is, does the lass have an interest in you?"

Conviction

"What do you think? Is this dress all right?" Vangie smoothed the material with her hands, turning to get another glimpse in the mirror while Suzette studied her.

"You look wonderful. Griff won't be able to take his eyes off you."

"I don't know why I'm so worried about how I look. It's not as if Griff is interested in courting me. He's simply joining us for supper. How did you get the evening off?"

Brushing a strand of hair from her face, Suzette sat down on the edge of the bed. "I'm giving Zeke more responsibilities. He's earned the chance to manage without me hovering all the time. Besides, I want to have a few more evenings off. Bay and I have had so little time together since the wedding."

Sitting next to her, Vangie reached over, taking her hand. "It's my fault you two didn't go to San Francisco as you'd planned."

"Nothing was your fault, and please don't think it was."

"Eustice arriving changed everything. Well, he's settled in his new shop, and I'll be moving to my own house shortly. Bay is talking to the owner of the one at the end of this block."

"Ah, yes. The man is rarely in town. From what I know, he has a business in San Francisco. August told me he's married, but no one has ever seen his wife." Pursing her lips, Suzette shrugged. "It would be wonderful if Bay can convince him to sell the house to you. If not, there's another one farther down the street, toward Eustice's shop. An older woman lives there, but her family wants to move her to their place in Sacramento."

Grinning, Vangie picked up a shawl slung across the bed. "How do you know all this, Suzette?"

"The restaurant. You might be surprised at what I learn after people have had a whiskey or wine. I've already told Bay about what her son and daughter-in-law said when they came here for a visit. Between them and the man from San Francisco, I'm sure you'll have your own house soon."

Standing, Vangie took one more twirl in front of the mirror, her smile fading a little. "I do like Griff, but from what you've said, he's quite the rake."

Stepping behind her, Suzette closed the one remaining button at the back of Vangie's dress. "He does enjoy spending time with beautiful women. Griff has been my friend a long time, and from what I've seen, he's always a gentleman. I'm certain Bay would tell you the same." Grasping her shoulders, Suzette turned Vangie around to face her. "How many times have we had supper here and Griff's been invited?"

"Quite a few since I've been in Conviction."

"You're having supper with three friends, nothing more. Don't worry so much."

"I know you're right. I'm making too much of this. It's just..."

"What?" Suzette asked.

Fidgeting with the sleeve of her dress, Vangie felt her face heat. "It's just, well...I keep hoping Cam will ask to escort me to supper. For a while, I believed he held an interest in me. He's had plenty of chances." Picking up her cup of cold tea, she lifted it to her mouth.

"You scare him."

Choking on the tea, she set the cup down. "Scare him? From what I've seen, nothing scares Cam. Quite the opposite." She shook her head. "It's all right, Suzette. I'm making too much of this. Wishing he would show an interest is simply a small fantasy. It's time I got out and met more of the people in Conviction. Between the kidnapping, your wedding, and Eustice arriving, I've been too busy to visit most of the shops. Starting tomorrow, I plan to start at one end of the main street and not stop until I visit every store."

"I want you to enjoy yourself tonight, Vangie."

Hugging Suzette, she stepped away. "That's exactly what I intend to do."

Circle M

Cam was the first to notice flames coming from the southernmost corral. Unable to sleep, he'd finally given up and headed outside around midnight. Sitting down, he closed his eyes, Bram's words parading through his mind.

Of all his cousins, he and Bram were the closest. The same age with a shared fondness for working horses, their bond had been immediate. More often than not, they'd been able to read the other's thoughts, feel when the other struggled with a decision.

If he hadn't been so focused on what Bram had said earlier, Cam might have noticed the fire sooner. Yelling as he ran toward the blaze, he grabbed two buckets, filling them while shouting to the others to do the same.

Reaching the corral, he tossed water onto the flames, disgusted at how little it helped. "Hurry, lads. We have to get it stopped before it reaches the barn."

Every MacLaren filled buckets or shoveled dirt. The two ranch hands not out with the herd joined them. They might have arrived earlier if the bunkhouse hadn't been located north of the four-house compound. It took close to half an hour to stop the fire, which had destroyed the fencing, but only charred the outside wall of the barn.

Wiping his hands down his pants, leaving trails of dirt and soot, Cam's jaw tightened as he surveyed the woods to the south. Dropping the shovel, he rushed to where Duke stood in a pasture at the other end of the compound. Whistling, he didn't need a halter for the palomino to follow him into the barn.

Within minutes, Cam swung into the saddle and charged from the barn. Ignoring the shouts from his family, he reined south toward the gypsy camp. He'd gotten a hundred yards from the last ranch house when a strong hand reached out, tearing the reins from his grasp.

Shouting curses, he lunged at Colin atop an unsaddled Chieftain, throwing them both to the ground. Hurling punches, they rolled around, anger flowing off them.

"Pull the lads apart," Ewan, the older of the two surviving uncles, yelled at the others. Bram and Fletcher grabbed Cam's legs, dragging him aside, while Quinn and Thane yanked Colin up, shoving him several feet away.

"What the hell are you lads doing?"

Swiping blood from his mouth, Colin glared at Cam. "The eejit planned to ride straight to the gypsy camp. *Alone*," he snarled.

"How would you know where I was going?" Cam stood, attempting to take a step closer when Bram and Fletcher yanked him back.

"Because we all feel the same. You'd be the only one addled enough to ride out without the rest of us."

"Addled, am I?" Pulling free, he rushed forward, dropping to the ground when Quinn's fist connected with his jaw.

"Enough!" Ewan passed a menacing glance between Colin and Cam.

"He shouldn't have tried to stop me." Rubbing his jaw, Cam accepted Bram's hand and stood.

Ewan moved to within inches of his nephew's face. "With your foul mood, one of the gypsies would've shot you. We've no proof they were the ones who set the fire. Everyone, get back to my house. We'll sort this out there."

Stomping off, Ewan mumbled under his breath and to his brother, Ian, who joined him on the walk back. "Those lads are too old to be rolling around in the dirt."

"Seems we did the same at their age, Ewan. Bloody noses, black eyes. Nothing serious. The lads will be over it by the time they get to your house."

"It's Cam I'm worried about. The lad's bothered by something other than the gypsies. It's been burning in him for weeks."

"If it's serious, he'll be talking to Bram. Those two are closer than any of the lads. With Fletch married, they're tighter than ever. We'll be figuring it out once we sort out the fire."

Walking inside, Ewan went straight to the cabinet, pulling out a bottle of whiskey and two glasses. Filling them, he handed one to Ian.

"We've a need for this before the lads arrive." Tossing it back, Ewan set the glass down. "And we both know it's the gypsies who set the fire. It's a matter of proving it before someone gets killed."

Chapter Six

Fletcher walked on one side of Cam, Bram on the other, neither allowing him to get more than a foot away. Fletcher nudged his shoulder.

"Colin was right to stop you, lad. If you'd gone on alone, I'm thinking you may not have made it back."

Glaring at him, Cam didn't respond, his anger still too fresh. Behind them, Colin carried on a quiet conversation with Quinn and Thane. If he hadn't let his rage control him, Cam knew he would've been included in the conversation.

"Are you ready to face the uncles and Colin, or do you want to stay outside?" Bram asked, figuring he knew the answer. The glare from Cam came in a split second.

"I'll not be left out." Stomping up the stairs, he shoved open the front door.

Several MacLarens were already inside, including Ewan's wife, Lorna, and Ian's wife, Gail. Colin walked in after him, his wife, Sarah, entering right behind him with their three-year-old son, Grant.

Everyone was there, including the younger children, and those the MacLarens had adopted—Coral, Opal, Pearl, and Jamie. The only family members missing were those no longer living at the ranch. Not one looked at Cam and Colin as if anything unusual had happened between them.

Ewan cleared his throat. "I've asked the ranch hands who aren't with the herd to guard the south area of the property."

"It was deliberate, Da."

"Ian and I are believing the same, Fletch. Brodie will be wanting proof." Ewan's gaze moved around the room. "Did any of you see anyone?"

"Everyone was inside except me, Uncle Ewan, and all I saw were the flames." Cam leaned down to brush dirt from his pants, wincing at Aunt Lorna's voice.

"Camden MacLaren, you'll not be dirtying my house. It's bad enough you and Colin got into a fight."

"Aye, Aunt Lorna. I'll not be doing it again."

Crossing her arms, she lifted a brow. "Dirtying my house or fighting with your brother?"

Cam shot a look at Colin. "The first. I'll not be promising something I'll not be able to keep."

A slight smile lifted the corners of Colin's mouth. "We need to speak of what we'll be doing next."

"Ian and I want you and Cam to ride out and bring back a couple more of our men. That should be leaving four with the herd."

Quinn stepped forward. "It may be best for Thane and me to ride out."

Ewan gave a quick shake of his head. "Nae. Colin and Cam will be going. All but the young lads and lasses will be rotating time, watching at night."

"I'll help."

Jamie's offer surprised no one. Since arriving at Circle M as a young boy and being adopted into the MacLaren clan, he'd done all he could to fit in.

"Aye, Jamie. You'll be taking watch, as will most of the family."

Shoulders relaxing a little, a slow grin crept across his face. "Can I ride out with Colin and Cam?"

"Not this time, lad," Colin replied. "We've got some things to work out."

The grin slipped a little before Jamie nodded.

"I'll be going to town tomorrow to speak with Brodie about tonight. The lad needs to be aware of the fire. And I'm in need of seeing my grandson." Ewan chuckled. "Lorna will be coming with me. We'll be passing the gypsy camp."

Taking a step forward, Fletcher shook his head. "Brodie won't be liking you and Ma going near them, Da."

"Aye, but I want to make certain the camp is still there. I'll not be riding close enough to anger them, and I'll not be putting your ma in danger.

"All right. We all have jobs and need a good night's sleep. Thane and Jamie, you lads will be taking the first watch."

"Thank you so much, Mr. Maloney. These are exactly what I wanted." Vangie clutched two dime novels against her chest. "I may come back for the other two."

"Don't wait too long, Miss Rousseau. These are quite popular." Maloney set the other books aside, totaling her purchase.

"Oh, all right. Please add those."

"You won't regret it. I'm expecting more books soon. Perhaps you'd want to stop by next week to see if they've arrived."

"I'll do that, Mr. Maloney. Thank you so much."

Sliding the books into the larger, drawstring bag, Vangie gave a short wave and left the store, a smile firmly in place. Suzette had been right to encourage her to attend supper the night before. Griff had been in good form, regaling them with stories of his youth. She hadn't laughed so much in a long time.

When supper ended, he'd escorted her home, tipping his hat before continuing to his house on the same street. He hadn't asked if he could escort her to lunch or another supper. As Suzette said, they were four friends sharing a meal, nothing more.

The two men who'd originally showed an interest in her no longer did. Vangie knew she wasn't ugly or had horrible manners. Her clothes were fashionable, if conservative, and unlike many women, she was financially secure. Vangie knew the real problem, although she'd never voiced it aloud.

"I'm boring," she whispered, continuing along the boardwalk.

Spotting Ferguson's Harness and Saddlery, Vangie stopped outside, staring through the large front window. Several saddles rested on racks, while bridles, halters, and reins filled the rest of the store. Heading to the door, she took a cautious step inside, cringing as the bell announced her presence. An older man entered from the back.

"Good afternoon, miss. May I help you?"

Her lips curved into a smile. "I was walking past and saw your lovely saddles through the window. I've been told you make everything here."

"My nephew, Deke, makes most of them these days. I'm Rube Ferguson. Are you looking for a new saddle?"

Running her hand over one with a more intricate design, she marveled at the beautiful workmanship. "I'm considering buying a horse. If I do, I'll need everything, including a saddle." Lifting her hand, she turned to look at the older man. "I apologize for my rude behavior. I'm Evangeline Rousseau."

"I've heard of you, Miss Rousseau. You're friends with Suzette Donahue."

Her brows lifted, though she kept her smile in place. "Why, yes."

"Conviction is growing, but in many ways, it's still a small town. You came to town not long before the kidnapping. Such a horrible thing to happen to a very nice woman. Thank goodness no harm came to her."

Vangie was tempted to disagree, knowing how much the ordeal affected Suzette. "She is doing quite well now." She turned when the bell over the door chimed.

"Deke. I'm glad you came back so soon. We have a potential customer. This is Miss Evangeline Rousseau. Miss Rousseau, my nephew, Deke Arrington."

"It's a pleasure, Miss Rousseau."

"And you, Mr. Arrington."

"I've work in the back I need to get to. Stop by anytime, Miss Rousseau."

Grinning, Deke watched his uncle's hasty retreat. "Excuse his quick departure. My uncle prefers to work quietly at his bench rather than speak with customers. Are you interested in a saddle, or is he assuming too much?"

Vangie's eyes lit with amusement. "I assure you it was my idea. Although I don't have a horse."

Crossing his arms, he grinned down at her. "No horse, but you want a saddle?"

"I know it sounds odd, but I only just made the decision to buy one when I stopped outside your shop."

"Not odd at all. Assuming you do plan to go ahead with purchasing a horse."

"I do." She turned toward the gorgeous saddle which drew her into the shop, setting her hand on the cantle. "Will this one fit any horse I buy?"

Expression sobering, Deke stepped beside her. "Yes, but it's also the most expensive saddle in the shop."

"It is for sale, isn't it?"

"Everything in here is for sale, Miss Rousseau." Running his hand over the leather, his features softened. "This is the best one I've ever made."

Vangie's chest squeezed at the longing in his voice. "Why don't you use it for your own?"

Pulling his hand back, Deke shook his head. "It's much too fine for me. You, however, would do it justice."

"Then consider it sold."

"It's such a beautiful saddle, Eustice. I can't wait for you to see it." The glee in her voice made him smile.

"You need a horse, Vangie."

"That's why I'm here. I thought you might have one to purchase."

Lips twisting, Eustice scrubbed a hand down his face, shaking his head. "None good enough for you.

60

Bay says the MacLarens have the best horses around. You should talk to one of them." A boy-like excitement showed on the man's face. "Your friend is Cam MacLaren. You should talk to him."

Vangie's body reacted immediately to the name, the muscles of her stomach fluttering. "He's quite busy."

"He'll talk to *you*, Vangie." Eustice leaned toward her, lowering his voice. "He's sweet on you."

"What?" She shook her head, placing a hand over her heart. "I'm certain you're mistaken."

"No. He likes you very much. I can tell." A self-satisfied expression brightened Eustice's face. "I can take you out there, Vangie."

The thought of seeing Cam again, if only for a few minutes, caused her chest to tighten. "I don't want to take you away from your work."

"I want to go. Everyone says they have the best ranch in the area. Bay says they have four houses and four barns for all the families." Looking over his shoulder at the work he had yet to complete, he rubbed a hand over his forehead. "I can work late tonight. Then we can go out there tomorrow."

"Well, if you're certain it won't put you behind."

Shaking his head vigorously, Eustice flashed her a grin of pure anticipation. "I can work early and late. We could ride out after breakfast. It will be fun."

As always, his excitement was contagious. "All right then. I'll be here at nine tomorrow."

Clapping his hands together, Eustice nodded. "The wagon will be ready."

Leaving the blacksmith shop, Vangie's heart couldn't stop racing at the idea of seeing Cam. At first, her reaction to the handsome rancher caused her a good deal of concern. Over the weeks, the concern had turned to something more. Vangie wished she knew what it was.

Chapter Seven

Circle M

Cam swiped an arm across his forehead, surveying the new fence. "We've made good progress this morning, Bram."

"Aye. We'll be done by sunset." Picking up another post, he positioned it in the hole before surrounding it with several inches of rocks from the nearby river.

Without a word, he and Cam filled the remaining depth with clay soil. Tamping it down, they added more soil and tamped again. Finishing, both straightened, Bram's attention focused on an approaching wagon.

"Visitors are coming." Bram nodded to the trail from town.

Turning around, Cam squinted, the corners of his mouth sliding upward. "It's Eustice Hadley and Miss Rousseau."

"Your lass?"

Cam flashed him a warning glare. "Vangie *isn't* my lass."

Bram didn't hide his grin. "She is if you're using her first name."

Ignoring his cousin, Cam took a few steps toward them, holding up his hand in greeting.

Stopping, Eustice held out his hand. "Good morning, Mr. MacLaren."

Grasping the large, calloused hand, Cam chuckled. "You're to call me Cam, remember?"

A flush crept up the large man's face. "All right, Cam."

His gaze moved to Vangie, his grin growing. "Good morning, Miss Rousseau."

"Mr. MacLaren."

"Vangie wants to buy a horse."

Cam's focus didn't sway from Vangie when he answered. "Is that so, Eustice?"

"She already bought a saddle from Deke."

Surprise etched his face. "You've already paid for a saddle?"

Straightening on the hard bench seat, Vangie squared her shoulders, ready for an argument. "I have. Mr. Arrington had the perfect saddle. I'm now looking for the perfect horse. Eustice assures me your family has the best animals for miles."

"In the entire area, Vangie," Eustice corrected.

"You'll not find better horses west of Colorado."

"That's quite a boast, Mr. MacLaren."

"Not if it's true, Miss Rousseau. You've not met my cousin, Bram."

Stepping forward, he tipped his hat. "Miss Rousseau. It's a pleasure to meet you."

"Mr. MacLaren. Do you gentlemen have time to show me suitable horses today, or shall I return another time?" Vangie found it hard to keep her expression neutral. She'd been hoping to find Cam at the ranch. With him standing a few feet away, she found it hard to speak without coming across as an older version of her mother. Her discomfort increased at the twitch of amusement on Cam's lips.

"Since you've come all this way, we'll not make you come back." Cam placed a hand on the seat of the wagon. "Unless you'd rather return to the ranch to see me, lass."

Eyes wide, her mouth parted on a startled, "What?"

Before Cam could answer, Bram touched his shoulder, nodding behind the wagon. A buggy approached, the man driving easy to recognize.

"It's August Fielder. I'm betting he's come to call on your ma."

Cam watched the buggy come closer. He didn't know how he felt about his mother being openly courted, even by the most eligible bachelor in Conviction. Although years had passed since his father, Angus, and Bram's father, Gillis, had been murdered, he wasn't quite ready to see his mother take up with another man. Not even one he liked as much as August.

"You know, lad, Aunt Kyla deserves some happiness. She could do much worse than August," Bram said.

Even though they kept their voices low, Vangie could pick out most of the conversation. She'd heard about the murders of the two eldest MacLaren men, how their deaths had devastated the entire family.

"Aye, she does. It's hard seeing her move on, leaving Da behind."

"She'll not be leaving him behind. I believe Aunt Kyla will always love Uncle Angus. I wish my ma would meet someone as fine."

"It wouldn't bother you for Aunt Audrey to marry again?"

Bram waved at August, thinking of the evenings his mother seemed so alone and lost. "Nae. I'd be happy for her."

Lifting his hand to return August's wave, Cam thought of his mother, how the life had all but drained from her after his pa's death. Even with so much family surrounding her, she often appeared lonely, searching for something. Or maybe someone.

"Good morning, Mr. Fielder."

"Hello, Cam, Bram." He pulled the buggy closer to the wagon, donning his hat. "Ah, Miss Rousseau and Eustice. Bay mentioned you might be coming to pay the MacLarens a visit. If I heard right, you've already purchased a saddle from Deke."

"Yes, I have. The MacLarens have offered to help me select a mount."

"You've come to the right place, Miss Rousseau. No one breeds better horses than the MacLarens."

Shifting in the seat, he turned his attention to Cam. "I've come to escort Kyla on a buggy ride." His tone indicated he wasn't seeking permission.

"I'm certain Ma will enjoy the company."

August studied him a moment before leaning closer. "Do you have a moment to speak with me, Cam?"

"Aye." Cam looked at Bram. "Would you mind showing Miss Rousseau the horses?"

"Nae. I'd be happy to give her my thoughts on which one to choose. Follow me, Eustice, Miss Rousseau."

Waiting until they were out of earshot, August motioned for Cam to climb up beside him. Slapping the lines, he slowly moved the buggy forward.

"I've already spoken to Colin about my intentions toward your mother. Has he spoken to you?"

"Nae. Colin has said nothing to me."

"Then I'll tell you the same as I told him. I care deeply about your mother, Cam. It's my intention to ask Kyla to marry me."

He didn't know quite how to respond. It wasn't as if he and the rest of the family hadn't expected it. Still, hearing August state it so clearly was a jolt.

"I understand how much you still miss Angus, but he's gone, son. My intention is to not take his place, but your mother is still alive and deserves to find love again. I hope to be the man she chooses to give it to her. Do you have an objection?"

Swallowing, he felt his muscles tighten, his jaw clench. It felt selfish and somewhat childish to deny his mother this chance. "Nae. You'll get no objection from me."

"Excellent." Continuing the slow pace, August looked ahead to see Kyla standing on the front porch, arms crossed. "She's very protective of her family."

A grim smile curved Cam's mouth. "Aye, she is. I'll be getting off here, Mr. Fielder."

"If it's not too much to ask, I'd like it if you called me August."

Extending his hand, he nodded. "I'm wishing you and Ma good luck, August." He grasped the older man's hand, then jumped down. Waving at his mother, Cam strode to the northernmost corral, his thoughts muddled.

Forcing himself to remember he wouldn't be losing his mother, another thought stopped him in his tracks, causing him to glance back over his shoulder. Would August expect her to leave the ranch, live in his large house in town? Cam didn't have to ask to know the answer.

Standing next to Vangie, Bram divided his attention between the two men atop the wagon as Cam climbed down, wondering at the somber expression on their faces. He could guess the subject of their discussion, understanding how Cam must feel about his mother moving on.

Any fool could see how much August loved Kyla, and most believed she felt the same. Although every member of the family liked and respected August, it was a different matter knowing he meant to take her away.

Kyla had always been the acknowledged leader of the four eldest female MacLarens. She never forced anyone to her way of thinking, letting a determined manner speak for her. Not having her on the ranch each day would be hard for everyone.

"Have you found the lass a horse, Bram?" Cam sauntered toward them, nodding toward the corral.

"Nae."

Vangie felt her body tense the closer Cam got. "You have such fine animals. It's hard to make a decision."

Stopping beside her so their arms almost touched, he looked at her. "Which are the ones you fancy, lass?"

Vangie pointed to a bay. "The mare in the corner, and the roan gelding."

"Two good choices. Bram, saddle the mare while I fetch Duke."

"Why would you saddle the mare?" Vangie directed the question to Bram.

"The lad will be taking you for a ride. When you return, I'll have the gelding ready. It's best to ride them before making a decision." Turning away, he headed to the barn.

Excitement rolled through her. The reason for coming to Circle M wasn't just to buy a horse. Vangie had wanted time alone with Cam, believing it wouldn't happen unless she made the first move.

Eustice hurried to catch up with Bram. "Can I help you?"

"Aye, lad." Grabbing a halter, he handed it to Eustice. "You could bring the mare into the barn."

Watching as Eustice headed into the corral, Vangie joined Bram. "Thank you for giving him something to do. He gets anxious if there's no work for him."

"I've not known the lad long, but he seems to be a hard worker."

"He is," Vangie said, thinking back to their time as children. "He's also honest. I'm afraid he wouldn't know how to tell a lie." She stopped when Eustice returned with the mare, a broad smile on his face.

"She's a good horse, Vangie."

"I believe you're right, Eustice." Hearing the sound of boots on the hard ground, she felt an odd constriction in her chest at the sight of Cam approaching with his palomino gelding, Duke. Walking to them, she stroked the animal's neck.

"He's so beautiful."

Laughing, Cam shook his head. "Aye. He is quite braw."

"Braw?"

"Handsome, lass."

"Oh. Then he is very braw, Cam."

"Here she is. Her name's Duchess." Bram handed the reins to Vangie. "Would you like a boost up, lass?"

Cam shouldered him out of the way. "I'll be doing it." Bending, he cupped his hands, holding them steady while she mounted the mare.

Gathering her skirt, she settled in the saddle. "Thank you."

Cam mounted Duke, glancing at Vangie. "Are you ready, lass?"

Sucking in a breath to steady the hammering in her chest, she nodded. "Yes."

Turning around, he waited for Vangie to come up beside him before taking a trail north. "We'll not be gone long. You'll be wanting to ride the other horse before making a choice."

Vangie glanced over at him, finding it hard to believe her luck at getting him alone, far away from anyone overhearing.

What she wanted to say was daring and bold for a woman such as herself. Vangie had become so tired of sitting aside, waiting for men to notice her. There'd been two who'd shown an interest back home, but her father hadn't been impressed with either, believing she could do better.

With her parents gone, no one stood in her way. She was free to show an interest in a man because she found him attractive, not because of his status. Cam MacLaren had fascinated her since the first time they'd met.

He'd been recovering from a gunshot wound, which stopped him from riding out with Bay and a group of other men to rescue Suzette from outlaws who'd taken her. After hours talking, Vangie knew enough to confirm her desire to spend even more time with him.

At first, he'd shown the same interest in her, even sitting next to her at the celebration of Bay and Suzette's marriage. Cam had even ridden into town to call on her. Instead of being alone, he'd walked into a conversation about Eustice's future in Conviction. A discussion resulting in the purchase of the livery.

Squaring her shoulders, she bit her lower lip, deciding it was better to forge ahead than keep her desires buried inside. Clearing her voice, she reined the mare as close to Duke as possible.

"Cam?"

"Aye, lass?"

"Do you find me attractive?"

Chapter Eight

Vangie would've laughed at the shock on Cam's face if she hadn't been so anxious about his answer. And too stunned at herself for asking the question.

Reining to a stop, Cam stared at her, eyes bulging from their sockets. Opening his mouth to reply, he closed it, then opened it again.

"I..." He glanced away, still too stunned to respond.

"It's a simple question." This time, her words held little of the bravado displayed earlier.

Gripping the reins tight enough for her knuckles to turn white, she waited. After several long moments without a response, her stomach plummeted. In her mind, no response was the same as a negative one.

Looking away, she forced a serene expression before meeting his disbelieving gaze. "I suppose it was a silly question. Are you ready to start back?"

Not waiting for him, she kicked the mare, determined not to let the humiliation at his lack of a reply show. Moving the mare into a gallop, she rode without thought, letting the air cool her heated face. Vangie hoped her embarrassed flush would disappear by the time she reached the barn.

"Vangie, wait."

Ignoring Cam's shout, she continued on, relief washing over her at the sight of houses up ahead.

When he caught up with her, he tried to grab the reins, cursing under his breath when she reined away.

"Vangie, hold up, lass."

Refusing to heed his command, she continued, reaching the first house before slowing the mare to a walk. Stopping outside the barn, she slid to the ground, handing the reins to Bram.

"What did you think of Duchess?"

"She's perfect." Vangie hurried on when Cam stepped next to her. "How much are you asking for her?"

Gripping her elbow, Cam attempted to guide her several feet away, not expecting her response. Digging in her heels, Vangie yanked her arm from his grasp.

"Excuse me, but I was speaking with your cousin."

"You'll be negotiating the price with me, lass," Cam said.

Crossing her arms, Vangie tried to step around him, but he blocked her path. "Fine. How much do you want for Duchess?"

Fisting his hands at his sides, he blew out a breath before quoting a number.

"It's a fair price. I have it in my reticule."

Cam took a reluctant step aside, watching as she walked to the wagon. Retrieving the money, Vangie didn't return to him. Instead, she handed the funds to Bram while Eustice removed the saddle and tack from Duchess, tying her to the back of the wagon.

"I'm ready, Vangie."

As uncomfortable as she felt, she smiled at Eustice, then looked at Bram. "Thank you for your help. She's going to be a wonderful mount." Meeting Cam's gaze, she forced a smile. "I appreciate you taking the time to ride out with me."

Not waiting for a response, she climbed onto the wagon seat, staring straight ahead as Eustice drove them away from the ranch.

Cam watched her leave, regret piercing a hole in his gut.

"Did something happen between you and the lass?"

Sparing a disgruntled glance at Bram, he returned his gaze to the wagon as it disappeared along the trail. "Aye."

"Will you be telling me what happened?"

Crossing his arms, Cam gave a curt shake of his head. "Nae."

Turning on his heel, he grabbed Duke's reins, stalking to the barn. Cam had no intention of sharing or explaining what Vangie asked when he didn't understand it himself.

First off, a woman didn't ask a man if he found her attractive. At least no woman he'd ever known. Her boldness had stunned Cam, rendering him speechless. Vangie had taken his hesitation in the wrong way, deciding his answer was *no*.

The second thing eating at him was the way she refused to listen to his explanation. Not that he blamed her. He'd been an idiot not to immediately tell Vangie he found her to be the most beautiful woman he'd ever known.

Brushing Duke, he blew out an unrestrained string of curses. "You're an eejit, Cam MacLaren."

"I've been saying that for years, lad." Bram stopped next to him, his broad smile meant to annoy his cousin. It worked.

"I've not asked your thoughts."

"Never said you did. Miss Rousseau is a real bonny lass. If you've no interest—" It was all Bram got out before Cam grabbed him by the front of his shirt.

"I'm warning you. Stay away from the lass."

Bram's deep laughter had Cam shoving him away. "Miscreant."

Not bothering with a halter, Cam whistled for Duke to follow him to the corral by the barn, muttering to himself. Closing the gate behind his horse, he leaned against it, lifting his face to the sky.

Vangie fascinated him more than any woman he'd ever known. Spending time with her always left Cam in a state of amused confusion, as well as a strong desire to see her again.

All morning while working with Bram, his mind had been on her, wishing he had time to ride into town and escort her to lunch or supper. The sight of her approaching in the wagon with Eustice unsettled and pleased him. The same reaction whenever he saw her.

Until today, Cam thought he had a good deal of time to express his interest in the enchanting woman. With a simple question, she'd flung his plans into the wind. It wasn't that he didn't have an answer. He'd been mesmerized by her beauty from the first moment they'd met.

Cam simply hadn't expected the quiet, unassuming woman to ask such a bold question. A question which would've been answered with a resounding *yes* if he'd been able to get the word out.

Instead, his mouth had gone dry, throat constricting to a point it ached.

"You'll need to be going after her, lad."

Cam spun to face his cousin, his own thoughts still muddled as to what he should do.

"Soon, lad. Whatever happened, the lass was a wee bit miffed at you when she and Eustice left."

There'd be no arguing with Bram. In fact, Vangie was a good deal more than miffed, although she'd done all in her power to hide it. Cam's lack of response had wounded her, which in turn had injured him.

"We've a good deal of work to do this week. I'll ride to town on Saturday to pay my respects."

"And apologize?"

Sucking in a deep breath, Cam's gaze moved to the trail toward Conviction. A major part of him wanted to resaddle Duke and go after her, explain his actions and hope she'd understand.

Instead, his boots remained rooted in place, responsibilities to the ranch weighing on him. He loved his family and their ranch. Since he was a young boy, he'd known his future lay in breeding cattle and horses. He'd always believed all the family thought the same.

Over the last few years, he'd watched as one MacLaren after another chose a different life or moved to pursue their own dreams. After the deaths of his father, Angus, and Uncle Gillis, his cousin, Brodie, had accepted the position as sheriff. His cousin, Jinny, an accomplished ranch woman, had married Deputy Sam Covington and moved to town.

His cousin, Heather, an expert rider and cattlewoman, had married Caleb Stewart and moved to Settlers Valley. Not long after, Cam's brother, Blaine, had taken on the role of foreman at the MacLaren property several hours north of Circle M. Another cousin, Sean, had been sent to Scotland to attend veterinary school. And soon, Thane might be joining Blaine on the ranch up north.

The responsibilities for those who stayed increased with each change. Cam didn't begrudge them their decisions. They were doing what made them happy, which was what he wanted for himself.

Now it appeared his own mother would be marrying August and moving to town. Which brought his thoughts back to Vangie and the real reason he'd delayed showing his interest.

Cam had always thought he'd marry a ranch woman. Someone like his mother, aunts, and cousins. Never had he imagined his interest would land on a city girl. A woman used to a refined life, including a housekeeper and cook. Not one including preparing meals for a large brood, days starting before sunrise, not ending until well past sunset.

It would be an incredible request of a woman as fine as Vangie. One he wasn't certain he could ask of her.

That was why he stood, back rigid, watching the trail to town. His mind wrestled with what was the wise decision while the rest of him fought his growing desire for Suzette Donahue's closest friend.

There was, however, one other consideration, and it was no small matter. At least two other men held an interest in Vangie. Suzette's assistant, Zeke Clayton, and Brodie's deputy, Seth Montero.

Both were fine men, respected and well-liked. And both lived in town.

No one knew much about Zeke's background, other than he'd traveled west to seek a position in a fine restaurant. He'd made it no farther than Conviction. It had taken Suzette less than an hour to hire him, and she'd never regretted it.

She paid him enough to rent one of the houses a block behind the restaurant, keep his horse stabled at Eustice's livery, and enjoy the fine clothes and food he preferred. According to Suzette, it wouldn't be long before he saved enough to buy his own home. An indication of his intent to stay in Conviction.

There'd been one woman he'd shown an interest in since arriving. Evangeline Rousseau. Cam had a strong sense Zeke had been holding back, waiting to learn Cam's intentions.

He believed the same of Seth Montero. Tall and lean with dark hair, piercing caramel eyes, and a brooding nature, the deputy had a reputation to rival Cam's cousin, Quinn, before he married Emma.

Seth was well-read, spoke several languages, and was a descendant of one of the founding families of California. It had been rumored he'd been a gun for hire in Texas at one time, giving it up after falling in love. As the story went, she'd died a week before their marriage, prompting Seth to return west.

Although most suspected Brodie knew the truth of Seth's past, he refused to confirm the stories. It was the reason so many trusted Cam's cousin. If he gave his word, there'd be no doubt Brodie would keep it.

No matter Seth's past, he was a man Cam admired, the same as he admired Zeke. Either man would be a better choice for Vangie than him.

Instead of going after her, voicing his interest, perhaps it was time Cam stepped aside, allowing Seth or Zeke, or both, an opening to court her. A ball of pain churned in his stomach, the same as it did each time he thought of Vangie with someone else. Yet he wanted what was best for her.

Step aside or voice his desire to court her. A decision which kept him up at night, consuming his thoughts each day. Her appearance at the ranch today, the question she'd asked, surprised him. It also revealed her feelings for him.

No longer did he have the luxury of time. He needed to make a choice, and it had to be made soon.

Chapter Nine

Belcher Grey sat across the campfire from Jean-Paul Heron, studying his distant cousin's movements. He knew no man as generous to the family or with as black a heart.

If a child needed a broken arm tended, Jean-Paul offered the knowledge and patience to set it. If a thief stole from any member of the family, Jean-Paul exacted justice without a hint of remorse. The same as he'd done in town when he'd located a man who'd shared their hospitality, then skulked away with a drawstring bag filled with coin.

It hadn't taken the sheriff long to visit the camp after the attempted robbery and killing of one of the thieves. Brodie MacLaren, the woman, and other men thought Belcher and his clan hadn't known why they visited. Before making camp, they'd learned all about the sheriff and his esteemed family of ranchers. Their trip had been wasted. They'd done nothing more than warm their hands and take furtive glances around the camp.

Waiting until certain the four wouldn't turn back, Jean-Paul emerged from the woods, the gun in his hand.

When Belcher asked him about the other robbers, Jean-Paul shrugged. He cared nothing about the other two, only the man who'd made the mistake of stealing from the family.

The gun he held tonight had been cleaned numerous times since he'd returned to camp after the shooting. Belcher had learned the local judge, August Fielder, had found the other outlaws guilty of attempted robbery and sentenced them to time in San Quentin.

"We should leave," Belcher said, not taking his gaze from the gun in the man's hand. Jean-Paul wasn't hotheaded, allowing anger to rule his actions. Many would think he was worse—a calculating killer without remorse.

The only people exempt from his wrath was family. The man who'd robbed them hadn't been family or he might've been spared. Doubtless *would've* been spared.

Jean-Paul made certain everyone had food, clothing, and medical care. He considered them harvesters most of the time, hunters when needed. The difference lay in the fact they harvested from what others planted and hunted cattle from ranches near where they camped.

If all went well, they'd stay in one place as long as six months. If not, they'd pack their wagons and ride out in the middle of the night. As far as Belcher and Jean-Paul were concerned, their current camp, less than a mile from Circle M, provided the perfect location.

Butchering one head of cattle would provide enough meat for weeks. They'd done it enough times to know, and the MacLaren cattle were considered the best for hundreds of miles. Rabbits, squirrels, vegetables—stolen of course—and fallen fruit from overladen trees rounded out their diet.

Flour, sugar, lard, and salt were purchased with money earned by telling fortunes, and obtaining short-term work on ranches or in nearby towns. Two of the men had already obtained work at saloons in Conviction.

Jean-Paul had plans to take four men tonight to cut a steer from the MacLaren herd and return it to their camp. Each person had a job and knew it well. Slaughtering the animal wouldn't take long. Neither would covering the evidence of what they'd done.

By the time the MacLarens arrived to question them, pieces of meat would be drying in the hidden back half of three wagons. In all the years they'd been stealing cattle, no one had ever discovered the false walls concealing the meat lockers.

Belcher tossed two more pieces of wood on the fire, leaning forward to rest his arms on his legs. "We should leave, Jean-Paul."

His work cleaning the gun completed, Jean-Paul holstered it, meeting Belcher's gaze. "It's too soon. We need meat, and there will not be a better chance than we have here."

"They aren't stupid. Once the MacLarens discover a steer is missing, they'll ride straight to our camp. The sheriff will come with his men. They won't be satisfied until they've torn our camp apart."

"There's nothing to find, Belcher."

A smirk curved his lips. "There will be if you slaughter one of their steers."

Jean-Paul stared into the fire. "We have no choice. We're low on meat. I'll take the men out tonight. By sunrise, we'll have what we need and there'll be no sign of what's been done."

Belcher tossed more wood on the fire, resigned to what would come next. The decision had been made. All he could do was prepare for the imminent confrontation and do everything possible to protect the family.

Conviction

Zeke sat alone at the table next to the restaurant's front window, sipping his first cup of coffee. The day had dawned with gray skies and a light drizzle, a surprise given the warm, sunny days of the last month.

He'd wrestled with a decision for weeks, unable to make a choice. Two bright, beautiful women had captured his attention.

One satisfied his need for a respectable, proper lady who'd welcome marriage and a family. The other fired his blood, yet offered none of the genteel propriety he sought.

Zeke had clawed his way from being a street urchin of five, living on handouts or what he could steal, to his current position as Suzette's assistant. It had been a difficult journey, one filled with humiliation and occasional praise. Good and bad men had passed through his life. Zeke did his best to learn from both types, fighting to keep the decency he'd found so difficult to achieve. The one constant had been Louella Dowling.

"Mr. Clayton, the kitchen staff is ready."

Pulling out his watch, he noted the time before nodding at the kitchen assistant. "I'll open the doors in two minutes."

"Yes, sir. I'll let the chef know."

Standing, he picked up the cup. No one stood outside waiting to enter. An odd occurrence for a restaurant which boasted a healthy number of daily diners. He didn't dwell on the thought. Instead, his mind returned to the two women.

Louella reminded him of the past he'd left behind. The other woman, a future he'd been seeking his entire life. Louella had followed him west, not giving up on them, even when he'd insisted they had no future. The second woman didn't even know of his interest.

Louella loved him with every part of her being, had been in love with him since they were children on the street, fighting together for every scrap of food or place to lay their heads at night. He couldn't count the number of times they'd fallen asleep in each other's arms to conserve warmth and create a false sense of security.

Over time, he'd pulled himself off the streets. Life had been harder for Louella. Despite his protests, she'd been forced to provide comfort to lonely men in the upstairs rooms of various saloons. It had sickened him to see her sell what he thought of as precious, worthy of protection.

Unable to watch her downward spiral, he'd left Louella behind, only to have her follow him months later. This time, she'd found work at the Gold Dust Hotel and Restaurant, cleaning rooms and serving meals.

Although she'd been the one to follow him, she kept her distance, as if unable to bear being away from him but no longer trusted his friendship. It broke his heart to know how much his leaving had hurt her. Still, he wasn't certain they'd be right together.

"We're ready, sir."

Handing his empty cup to the man, Zeke straightened his jacket. Stepping forward, he released the lock, pulling the door wide. Eyes widening, his breath caught.

Outside, Louella stood with her arm tucked through the arm of a handsome young man in dark gray pants, black coat, shiny black boots, and a crisp, black Stetson. What startled him most was the brilliant smile on her face. A smile Zeke hadn't seen in a very long time.

Suzette stood from where she'd been penning a letter to a friend back east, a small glass of brandy nearby. Across the room, Vangie, legs tucked beneath her, worked on a complicated needlepoint.

After supper, Bay had left for a meeting, leaving the women to their own interests. Suzette had worked six hours at the restaurant, arriving at ten to relieve Zeke, leaving when he returned at four. They'd been experimenting with these hours for a week, and so far, both were happy with the change.

Setting down her pen, she turned toward Vangie. "Let's go for a ride early tomorrow morning. I haven't seen your horse. What's her name?"

"Duchess, and she's a beautiful bay mare."

"Have you ridden her?" Suzette asked.

"A short ride with Cam. Long enough for me to decide she was what I wanted. I'd love to go for a ride with you tomorrow."

"It will have to be early, as I must be back in time to change clothes and get to the restaurant by ten."

Taking another sip of brandy, Suzette set the glass down. "Did Cam ask about taking you to supper?"

"No."

Brows drawing together at the clipped response, Suzette moved to sit beside her. "What happened?"

Setting down the needlepoint, Vangie bit her lower lip, still embarrassed at the question she'd asked Cam. "Nothing happened. He doesn't have an interest in me. None whatsoever."

Suzette didn't believe it, but wouldn't voice that now. She'd rarely seen a man who signaled his interest in a woman as openly as Cam did with Vangie.

"He's probably busy. There's so much to running a ranch. The MacLarens work sunrise to sunset, you know."

Unable to hold back, Vangie let out a mirthless laugh. "I do have *some* concept of the amount of work required to run a ranch. Believe me, this isn't about too many chores. Cam doesn't have an interest in me."

"How do you know that?"

"Because I asked him," she blurted out.

"*What?*"

Gaze shifting away, she gave a slight shake of her head. "I asked him if he found me attractive. He didn't answer. Not a single word." She felt her face heat, the same as it had riding atop Duchess.

"I'm sorry, Vangie. I was certain Cam held an interest in you."

Shrugging, she picked up the needlepoint, feigning interest in the intricate pattern. "It's all right. At least I know his feelings."

Picking up Suzette's glass, she took a sip, wincing. "Oh my. How can you drink that?"

Smiling, Suzette took the glass from her. "It's an acquired taste. You need to build up to it slowly."

At a loud knock, Vangie's gaze shot to the front door. "Are you expecting visitors?"

"No." Standing, Suzette drew the door open. "Deputy Montero. What a nice surprise. Please, come in."

Removing his hat, Seth stepped inside, spotting Vangie right away. "Miss Rousseau."

Standing, she walked toward him. "It's good to see you, Deputy. May I get you a drink? Whiskey, brandy, coffee?"

"Nothing, thank you."

Stepping next to him, Suzette indicated a chair. "Please, sit down."

"I don't have time tonight. Brodie asked me to come by and let you know we might have some information on those two men Eustice talked about."

This got their attention. Vangie's back stiffened, mouth going dry. "What have you learned?"

"Sam Covington suggested Brodie contact the sheriff in Grand Rapids. Turns out the description Eustice gave us matches two men the sheriff and his men have been looking for."

"What'd they do?" Suzette asked.

"Grand larceny. Which falls in line with what Eustice told us about them."

Vangie cocked her head. "Eustice said the men were looking for my father because he owed them money."

"The sheriff in Grand Rapids says there are several complaints against the men for fraudulent investments. He doesn't know anything about your father owing them money."

Vangie's shoulders slumped. "You said the sheriff was searching for them."

"Seems they disappeared."

Color draining from her face, Vangie took a couple shaky steps and sat down. "Disappeared?"

"Sorry, Miss Rousseau. I know it doesn't comfort you, but at least we know what Eustice said could be true. And we now have their names. Merle and Reggie Riordan."

Chapter Ten

Putting a hand to her mouth, Vangie sent a panicked glance at Suzette before running from the room.

"Is she all right?" Seth asked, moving toward the kitchen where Vangie disappeared.

Worry lines etched Suzette's face. "I don't know." Moving past him, she followed Vangie, finding her leaning over the sink, losing the contents of her stomach. Grabbing a rag, she dampened it, pressing the cloth against her forehead.

A moment later, Vangie raised her head, sucking in a slow breath. "Sorry."

"There's nothing to apologize for. I would like to know what caused you to lose your supper."

Turning, her cheeks burned at the sight of Seth leaning against the doorjamb. Straightening, she slid her hands down the front of her skirt, trying to regain her composure.

"Are you certain you have the correct names?"

Seth shot a quick look at Suzette before nodding. "Yes. Do you know them?"

Another wave of nausea assailed her, but she forced it aside. "Yes. They came to the house before my parents died, asking for my father. My mother and I were on our way out, but I remember their names."

"Do you know why they wanted to see your father?" Seth asked.

Lips drawing into a thin line, she shook her head. "No."

"It's still good information. I'll let Brodie know. The connection between them and your father is important. Especially after what Eustice said about them." Shoving away from the door, he took a step forward. "We have their descriptions and names. If they're stupid enough to come to Conviction, they won't be able to get too close to you."

The heavy pressure in her chest began to ease. "Are you saying that to make me feel better, or do you believe it?"

The corners of his mouth twitched before his features sobered. "No one is going to let anything happen to you."

"All right."

"I'd best get back to the jail." He gave Suzette a nod before turning away, noticing Vangie following. Reaching the door, he pulled it open.

"Thank you for letting us know about the Riordans, Deputy."

Stepping outside, he settled the hat on his head, then turned back. "If you don't have plans, I'd be honored to escort you to lunch tomorrow, Miss Rousseau."

Surprise washed over her. She'd never suspected the tall, olive-skinned, quite handsome deputy held any interest in her. The humiliation of her encounter with Cam began to fade at the interest on Seth's face.

"That would be lovely, Deputy Montero."

A devastating smile, one he'd probably used with many women, transformed his serious features. "I'll call for you a little before noon tomorrow. Have a good evening, Miss Rousseau."

"You as well, Deputy Montero."

Salt Lake City

Merle Riordan tossed back the whiskey, picking up the bottle to replenish his glass. His bleary gaze took in the ramshackle saloon located at the end of town which provided drinks not offered in the Mormon section.

He and Reggie were trail weary. Stagecoach travel held none of the adventure the ticket sellers spoke of, leaving them sore and depleted of energy after several long days. Reaching the growing Utah town, they'd departed the stage, deciding a couple nights in a regular bed, consuming decent food, was in order.

Reggie stood at the bar, peppering the bartender with questions about Eustice. Merle could tell the tall, burly looking man hadn't seen the blacksmith and had grown tired of being interrogated by someone he didn't know. When the man walked away to help another customer, Reggie gave up and returned to their table.

Plopping into a chair, Reggie filled his empty glass. "He hasn't seen him."

"Didn't expect him to. Eustice isn't a drinker. No reason for him to stop in at a saloon. We might have better luck in the restaurants, but that would entail several days. Besides, the stage driver remembered him and swore Eustice was headed to California. If we just knew to where." Merle shrugged, more than ready to move on from this conversation. To put the entire trip behind them and return to Grand Rapids. Reggie wouldn't hear of it. They'd come this far and wouldn't go home until they'd found Evangeline Rousseau and reclaimed their money.

Still thinking it a fool's journey, Merle continued to make his point clear, knowing Reggie would ignore his wishes. They were in this to the end. He just hoped the end didn't include them going home in pine boxes.

Circle M

"Where are you going, lad? It's not even noon on a Saturday." Bram crossed his arms, their cousin, Fletcher, standing next to him, smirking.

Cam ignored both, grabbing his gunbelt from the dresser in his bedroom, securing it around his hips. Checking his boots, he bent down, rubbing them with the sleeve of his shirt.

"Aunt Kyla's not going to be happy about you ruining your shirt." Bram winked at Fletcher.

"I'm guessing the lad will be going to town to see a bonny, red-haired lass. Is it true, lad?" Fletcher asked.

Picking up his hat, he shot his cousins a hard glare. "Ma knows where I'm going."

"And that would be?" Bram asked.

"To town."

"It's past time you made your intentions toward Miss Rousseau known." Bram's earnest comment had Cam stalling. It had taken him almost two days to talk himself into approaching Vangie. Two days of comparing himself to Zeke and Seth. Even though he still felt she'd be better off with a man comfortable in town, he couldn't get her out of his head.

The sassy question about finding her attractive excited him as much as it confused him. He chuckled each time he thought of her bold query. Too bad he hadn't been able to answer Vangie when the question left her lips. If he'd only said *yes*, he wouldn't feel as if he had to climb out of the deep hole he'd dug for himself.

"Are you going to invite the lass to lunch?" Fletcher hadn't been married long and was still getting used to having a wife and a baby son. He loved Maddy and Dylan with all his heart, showing no sign of envying his unmarried cousins' ability to visit the lasses in saloons. He hadn't been inside one in months and didn't miss it.

"Aye. If she has plans for lunch, I'll ask to accompany her to supper."

Dropping his arms to his sides, the corners of Bram's mouth tilted upward. "The lass won't be having plans, lad. For some reason, she's smitten with you."

Fletcher shook his head. "Nae. The lass is in love with him. I'm wondering what she thinks about how long it's taken him to do something about it."

"You're both eejits."

Tiring of the conversation, Cam shoved past them into the upstairs hall. Taking the stairs, he joined his mother in the kitchen, watching as she poured hot water off the boiled potatoes.

"I'll be leaving now, Ma."

Turning, she dried her hands on her apron before stepping forward. "It's a good thing you're doing, Camden. Vangie Rousseau is a bonny young lass." Getting on her toes, she kissed his cheek.

Glancing over his shoulder to make sure Bram and Fletcher weren't listening, he fingered the brim of his hat. "I'm not certain it's a good decision. She's a town lass, Ma."

"You won't be knowing her heart until you spend time with her. Seeing her today doesn't mean you'll be marrying the lass. You're too far ahead of yourself, lad."

97

Chuckling, he nodded. "Aye. You're right."

Studying her face, Cam pondered asking the question which had haunted him since August rode to the ranch the day Vangie bought the horse.

"Is there something worrying you, lad?"

"I've a question, Ma."

Pulling out a chair, she sat down, motioning at the seat next to her. "All right. Tell me what's been bothering you." The way she said it indicated she might already know what weighed on him.

Lowering himself into the chair, he set his hat on the table. "August Fielder."

A knowing look crossed her face, features softening. "What about August?"

"He wants to marry you."

"Aye, he does."

A wave of loss hit him before he shoved it aside. "Will you be marrying him?"

Clasping her hands together on top of the table, she leaned toward him. "Aye. I've already told him I will. We plan to tell everyone tomorrow at Sunday supper." Sitting back, her gaze moved over his solemn features. "Do you have objections to us marrying?"

Instead of answering, he asked a question of his own. "Do you love him, Ma?"

Moving her hands to her lap, she glanced around the kitchen, as if seeking an answer. After several long moments, she met his gaze.

"Aye, I do love August, but it's not the same love I felt for your da. I'll never be loving another man as I did Angus. August understands this and still is wanting to marry me. He's a good man, Camden. Honest, smart, kind, with a big heart." Brushing a strand of hair from her forehead, she let the silence stretch another moment. "I've no doubt he'll be faithful to me."

"Aye, Ma. I'm believing he will be."

"But that's not what's troubling you, lad. Tell me."

Looking away, Cam wished he'd never shown his concern. This was a discussion he should be having with his brother, Colin, and his wife, Sarah, before speaking of it to their mother.

"You might as well tell me, Camden, or we'll be sitting here until you do."

"Will you be moving to town?"

Chuckling, she shook her head. "Aye and nae. I'll be staying here with August some nights and at his house in town the other nights. We've not settled on days, but he knows I won't be leaving the ranch behind. It's in my blood, the same as it's in yours."

Relief drifted through him, allowing Cam to let out the breath he'd been holding.

"Is that what you needed to hear?"

Reaching out, he covered her hands with his large one. "Aye, Ma."

"Colin and Sarah already asked the same of August. That's when he assured them we'd be having two homes." She grinned. "Imagine me living in two houses."

Squeezing her hands, he stood. "You deserve to be happy, Ma. If August loves you and makes you happy, then I'm glad you'll be marrying him."

Kyla stood, a wistful expression appearing. "I loved your da with all my heart. Even in death, my braw husband has it with him. I'll be missing him every day. Still, I'll be a good wife to August, and will be making him happy."

"I'm hoping you grow to love him, Ma. Da wouldn't want you to keep all your love for a man who can no longer return it."

A lone tear welled in her right eye. "Do you think so, Camden?"

Bending, he kissed her cheek. "Aye, Ma. I'm certain of it."

Chapter Eleven

Conviction

Cam continued to feel a deep sense of relief as he entered town. He'd been surprised Colin had already spoken to their ma about August and where they'd be living. His brother hadn't mentioned it to him, which stung. Vowing to speak with Colin about it, he rode to Bay's house and dismounted.

A ripple of unease assailed him as he took the steps to the front door. He'd never been nervous about talking to a woman. Then again, he'd never courted a woman before, certainly not one he'd offended.

Knocking, he took a step back, removing his hat when the door opened. "Good afternoon, Suzette. Is Vangie home?"

Surprise flashed across her face before she cleared her throat. "She isn't here right now, Cam. Did she know to expect you?"

Fingering the brim of his hat, he shook his head. "No. Do you know if the lass will be returning soon?"

Fighting what she should say versus what she wanted to say, Suzette opened the door, motioning him inside. "Please, sit down. I'll get you a cup of coffee."

Lowering himself onto the sturdy sofa against one wall, his gaze took in the room. Most of the furniture seemed too delicate and fine for a man of his size. He wondered where Bay sat. He wondered more where Vangie was, and if she'd be returning soon.

"Here you are." Suzette handed him the coffee, taking a seat in a chair across from him.

Taking a sip, he leaned back. "Do you know where she is?"

Clasping her hands in her lap, an uncomfortable look passed across her face. "Deputy Montero escorted her to lunch."

The excellent coffee turned to a stale gulp as her words sank in. He knew Seth held an interest in her. It was the reason he'd decided to heed Bram's warning and ride to town. A rancher and city woman might not be the perfect combination, but Cam decided not to hide his interest any longer.

"I was just going to prepare lunch for myself. Come into the kitchen and I'll prepare enough for both of us."

"I won't be putting you out, Suzette."

Standing, she waved him off. "Don't be ridiculous. There's plenty, and I'd rather not eat alone."

His appetite had fled the moment she mentioned Seth, but he refused to be rude. Shooting a glance at the front door, he followed, pacing to the back window of the large kitchen to look outside. Several more streets lined with houses were north of Bay's home.

"Seth stopped by yesterday to let us know Brodie learned the names of the two men after Vangie."

Whirling around, he walked to her. "Who are they?"

"Reggie and Merle Riordan. The sheriff in Grand Rapids is looking for them on charges of fraud, but they've disappeared." She set two plates filled with stew on the table, adding a bowl of biscuits.

Cam pulled out a chair for Suzette before taking a seat across the table. He didn't pick up the fork.

"Do they have any idea where they went?"

"Not according to what Seth told us."

He thought on that while scooping up a forkful of stew. Picking up the coffee, he swallowed, wondering if the Grand Rapids sheriff had sent Brodie descriptions. "Did they put out wanted posters on them?"

"Sorry, Cam. I don't know any more than I've told you."

"How did she take the news?"

"Not well. I think that may be why Deputy Montero asked her to lunch."

Cam would've laughed if his mouth wasn't full of food. Seth wasn't offering comfort as much as poaching on another man's woman. At least that was how Cam viewed it, which made no sense. The deputy was doing what Cam should've done long before now.

"I'll be speaking to Brodie when I leave here."

They stilled at the sound of the front door opening and closing. "Are you home, Suzette?"

Cam's stomach clenched at the familiar voice.

"In the kitchen, Vangie."

Setting down the fork, he pushed from the table, standing to face the doorway. When she entered, he didn't miss the stunned expression or way she stiffened at the sight of him.

"Good afternoon, Vangie."

She relaxed a little at the use of the preferred nickname. It sounded so much better than the way he'd been so formal when she'd traveled to Circle M. She'd matched his formality, but didn't want to continue it here.

"Hello, Cam. I didn't expect to see you again." Seeing his brows furrow, she amended her response. "At least not so soon."

Removing her bonnet, she set it aside, eyeing the empty plates on the table.

"Cam stopped by to escort you to lunch." Suzette stood, picking up the dishes. "I told him you'd already left with Deputy Montero. Did you have a good time?"

Irritated Suzette had been so open with Cam, she forced a broad smile. "It was lovely. He's quite charming and a real gentleman."

It wasn't meant as a jab at Cam...at least not in a malicious way. That was what Vangie told herself before lifting a cup from the shelf and filling it with what was left of the coffee.

"He invited me to Sunday supper at the Gold Dust."

Suzette leaned a hip against the counter. "Did you accept?"

"Of course. He's quite entertaining."

Cam just bet he was, but didn't comment. The two women spoke as if he wasn't in the room. And maybe he shouldn't be. She seemed genuinely interested in Seth, a good, honest man Cam liked and respected.

"Thank you for lunch, Suzette. It's time for me to head back to the ranch."

"Will you be stopping to talk with Brodie?" Suzette asked, ignoring the stunned expression on Vangie's face.

"Aye. It was good to see you both." Skirting around Vangie, he grabbed his hat from a table before heading to the door.

"Wait, Cam."

His hand stilled on the knob. He didn't turn around, sensing Vangie step beside him.

Back rigid, she threaded her fingers together, ignoring the knot of fear in her chest.

"What is it, lass?"

She bit her lower lip. "I was wondering if you truly did come by to invite me to lunch."

"Aye. And to apologize for what happened at the ranch."

"Oh." She looked away, still feeling the humiliation at both her question and his lack of an answer. "It's all right. I'd never want you to lie about something as trivial—"

His hand grasping her chin stopped whatever else she meant to say. "Not trivial, Vangie." Letting go, he took a step away to stop himself from wrapping an arm around her waist and pulling her to him.

"Uncalled for then," she said.

Chuckling, he gave a slight shake of his head. "Nae. It was surprising. I've never had a lass ask me such a question."

Feeling her face heat, she pursed her lips. "I shouldn't have asked."

"I should've given you an answer."

Unable to stop herself, she touched his arm. "What would you have said?"

Opening his mouth to answer, Cam stopped at the sharp rap on the door. Shoulders slumping, Vangie reached out, drawing it open, and gasped.

Eustice, his face and clothes bloody, stood slightly bent over, Seth behind him. His eyes widened when he saw who moved to stand next to Vangie.

"Afternoon, Cam."

"Seth. What happened?"

Vangie reached out, grasping one of Eustice's hands. "First, come inside and let me take care of the cuts."

"It doesn't hurt, Vangie," Eustice said, but didn't resist her attempt to lead him into the parlor.

"Oh my." Suzette took one look and hurried back into the kitchen, returning with a damp cloth and bottle of whiskey.

"I don't want to get your nice chair bloody."

"Stay right where you are, Eustice, while Vangie and I take care of you." Suzette looked at Seth. "Who did this?"

"Three cowboys. They'd spent a couple hours in the Monarch, the new saloon that opened a few weeks ago. They were drunk when they left and headed to the livery. I don't know what started it, but according to a witness, the three started shoving Eustice around. When he didn't respond, they started beating him up."

Cam narrowed his gaze on Eustice. "Why didn't you defend yourself?"

"I didn't want to hurt them."

A slight smile appeared on Seth's face before his expression sobered. "Alex and I heard the commotion. Sam joined us a couple minutes later. They're taking the three to jail. Eustice refused to go to the clinic, so I brought him here."

Vangie gave him a warm smile before continuing to carefully clean the blood from Eustice's face. "You did the right thing, Deputy."

"Seth," he said.

"Right. Seth."

Anger at the simple exchange coursed through Cam, but he pushed it aside. "Do you know any of them, Eustice?"

"Their horses are at the livery. I don't know why they got mad at me." He looked at Vangie. "I was nice to them."

"I'm certain you were. Alcohol sometimes makes men act crazy." Rinsing out the cloth while Suzette dabbed his wounds with whiskey, she carefully finished removing the last of the blood. "What will happen to the men, Seth?"

"Brodie will decide after they spend the night in jail. He'll want to talk to Eustice." He looked down at him. "You are going to press charges, aren't you?"

"I don't want to cause trouble."

"You aren't the one who started it, Eustice," Seth said. "It's up to you, but they should at least pay for the damage to the livery."

"What did they do?" Cam asked.

"Tore tack and tools from the walls," Seth said. "Threw some of it into the forge before breaking a bench. That's what Alex and I witnessed when we arrived."

Cam crouched next to Eustice. "Seth is right, lad. You need to get paid for the damages."

"Is he right, Vangie?"

Setting the cloth into the bowl, she stood. "Yes, Cam and Seth are both right."

"I'd better get back to the jail." Seth started to turn, then stopped. "Is supper tomorrow still all right with you, Vangie?"

Cam wanted to land a blow to Seth's chin. Instead, he fisted his hands at his sides, waiting for her response.

"Of course."

"Good. I'll call on you at three." Seth didn't spare Cam a glance before leaving.

Studying Vangie's face, Cam didn't see the spark of interest in the deputy he'd expected. "Is he courting you, Vangie?"

Straightening, she dried her hands on a towel. "Would it bother you if he were?"

Jaw clenching, he felt the muscles in his back and shoulders tighten. "Aye, lass. It would."

Chapter Twelve

Five days had passed since Cam left Vangie, returning to Circle M. He'd said nothing about seeing her again or the upcoming supper with Seth. Her disappointment was acute.

Bay had invited Griff to the house for supper one night, entertaining them with stories of the two men when they were boys. Another night, Zeke had come by to speak with Suzette about a work matter. There'd been no more visits from Seth, although Vangie had heard Brodie sent him to Sacramento.

Confused at Cam's odd behavior and bored with nothing to do, she'd again stated her desire to buy her own house. The following day, Bay had prepared the purchase agreement for a house down the street from him and Suzette.

Her excitement spilled over the instant she added her signature to the document. "I can't quite believe I'll own my own home. A year ago, I wouldn't have considered the idea." The enthusiasm waned a little, realizing the death of her parents had allowed her to become an independent woman.

"It's a smart decision, Vangie. The house is in good repair and you bought it at a fair price." Bay placed the agreement aside, resting his arms on the edge of the desk. "You can move in whenever you'd like. Griff and I will be glad to help you on Saturday."

Vangie thought of what she owned and chuckled. "I only have what I brought with me from Grand Rapids, so it won't take long."

"You're fortunate the house comes with some of the furniture you'll need."

"Eustice can make what else I need. Suzette told me about a warehouse at the docks that houses furniture left behind when people leave the area. She says the owner asks fair prices as long as the buyer doesn't need help removing it from the warehouse."

"Stein Tharaldson, the owner of the feedlot and ranch supply store, also owns the warehouse. He's a good man and will offer an honest price. Griff and I will be happy to pick up whatever you buy. Have you met Stein?"

"I don't believe so."

Standing, he walked around the desk and grabbed his hat. "The supply store is just down the street. I'll introduce you and see if he has time to show you what he has. Afterward, I'll take you to the Feather River Restaurant for lunch. Suzette will be there, and I'm hoping she can join us."

Walking to the door, she smiled. "That would be wonderful. I don't have much money with me now."

"If you find something you want, Stein will take my word you're good for the cost." Letting August know he'd be gone a while, Bay stopped at Griff's office. "Vangie and I are going to Stein's to look at the furniture in his warehouse."

"I'll come with you. I'm in the process of buying the house next to Vangie's and need to start buying furniture." Grabbing his hat and adjusting his gunbelt, he joined them before the three headed down the stairs.

"Have you heard any more about the Riordan brothers?" Griff held the front door open for them.

Bay shook his head. "Nothing more. Brodie sent telegrams to sheriffs in several towns along stagecoach routes. The sheriff in Grand Rapids also sent word out."

The two men flanked Vangie as they walked to the end of the boardwalk, crossing the wide expanse of open area on their way to the supply store.

"Brodie has his deputies on alert and has the bartenders watching for men matching their description," Bay said. "Same with the hotels and the boardinghouse. My guess is we won't locate them before they arrive in Conviction."

"Which means Vangie shouldn't move out of your place until after Brodie has them in jail," Griff said.

Vangie stopped in front of the lumber mill. After a moment, Bay and Griff realized she was no longer with them and turned back.

"I'm going to move into my house on Saturday, whether those men have been found or not."

Resting his hands on his waist, Bay stared down at her. "Griff's right. If they learn you're living alone, it will make it much easier for them to get to you."

"Both you and Suzette work during the day, which means I'm alone at your house all the time."

"It's the nights I'm worried about, Vangie. You'll be alone in the new house with no one to help you if those two miscreants show up." Bay looked at Griff for help.

"You could stay in your new house during the day and sleep at Bay and Suzette's. You'll probably have supper with them most nights anyway."

Mouth twisting, she let out a slight huff of irritation. "It's not the same, Griff."

"But it's safer for you, which is what we should focus on, Vangie."

"It wouldn't be for long," Bay said. "You know Suzette will agree with me."

"As will August," Griff added.

Crossing her arms, she glared at them. "Now you're uniting against me?"

A slight smile lifted one corner of Bay's mouth. "If that's what it will take to get you to see reason, I'm fine with it."

"Me too," Griff smirked.

Frustrated, she dropped her arms, moving past them to the supply store. "I'll think about it." She tossed the words over her shoulder, continuing inside.

"What does it mean when a woman says she'll *think about it*?" Griff watched her disappear inside.

Bay barked out a laugh. "Not a *yes*, but not a *no*."

Following her, Griff rubbed fingers along his brow. "That is why I've never married. I don't get people who don't understand logic."

"They understand logic, all right. Just not the kind we do."

Sacramento

From his location outside the sheriff's office, Seth watched the two men enter the restaurant. They'd caught his attention when they'd passed by, arguing loud enough for anyone to hear. Both wore rumpled clothing, as if they'd traveled days, maybe weeks.

What kept Seth interested was the similarity in their appearance. Average height, a little overweight, sallow complexions, brown hair curled above the collar of their shirts. He'd bet they were related.

Following, he entered the same restaurant, spotting them being seated at a table against the far wall. Taking a chance, he walked forward and held out his hand to one of them.

"Tom James, right?"

Cocking his head, the man gave him a puzzled expression. "No. I don't believe we've ever met."

Dropping his hand to his side, he didn't move away. "Sorry about that. You look just like someone I know from back east. You two from around here?"

"No. We just arrived on the stage."

"Hope you didn't have to travel too long. Those stagecoaches can be brutal."

The other man spoke up. "Three weeks of traveling, and I'm not looking forward to the return trip."

Seth feigned a smile. "Coming all this way just to turn around and head back. A grueling journey for anyone."

"It wasn't bad when we took the train to St Louis. But the stage..." The man's voice trailed off before he clamped his mouth shut at the scowl from the other man.

"Well, I'll leave you two to your meal."

When he was a good distance away, the younger man, Wayne, leaned forward, lowering his voice. "Now that was odd. I don't believe the man thought he recognized you at all, Jeffrey. In any case, I don't see a reason not to engage in conversation with others."

"Because we cannot trust anyone. We're not to draw attention to ourselves until we've completed what brought us west."

"If you ask me, you've taken the secrecy much too far," Wayne said, forking a piece of meat as he watched Seth stroll by the front window of the restaurant.

Seth continued down the boardwalk to the sheriff's office. Entering, he looked around, finding no one. Waiting as long as he dared before heading outside, he made his way across the street to watch the restaurant entrance. An hour later, the men emerged.

Instead of walking toward the stage office, they headed to a small hotel near the restaurant. The same hotel where Seth had a room. Waiting a minute, he followed, looking around the inside. Seeing neither man, he stepped to the counter.

"A couple men just came in. I believe I know them." Seth described them, seeing recognition on the clerk's face.

"They have a room upstairs." The young man stared at the register. "Room sixteen. You can head up if you want."

Seth gave a quick shake of his head. "I don't want to bother them. Those are the Riordan brothers, right?"

Brows furrowing, the clerk took another glance at the register. "Nope. They registered under the name of Tipton. Jeffrey and Wayne."

"Huh. Guess I was mistaken. Sorry to bother you." Leaving, Seth headed straight to the telegraph office.

Cam finished working a young horse, swiping sweat from his brow as he led the colt to another corral. The last few days had been long. They'd discovered a couple head of cattle missing. There'd been no sign of a carcass, so they may have wandered off, or as Colin believed, were stolen.

They'd spent a good portion of the night before discussing options. Quinn and Fletcher agreed with Colin that they should ride to the gypsy camp. Uncles Ewan and Ian disagreed, wanting to wait until another search had been completed.

Colin, Thane, and a couple ranch hands had scoured the area for hours, moving in ever widening circles until accepting the cattle were gone. When they returned, the decision had been made to watch the gypsy camp, but not approach. Ewan and Ian preferred to have some kind of proof they'd taken one or both head. In the meantime, Thane had been sent to let Brodie know of their intentions.

They didn't request he join them. Instead, Ewan would send word to Brodie if they found evidence the gypsies had stolen the cattle.

Walking to the trough, Cam splashed water over his head and face. It had been almost a week since he'd seen Vangie. He'd wanted to return sooner after leaving without voicing his intentions. It had been a foolish decision for him to ride away without letting her know he intended to court her.

Although Cam thought the deputy a good choice, Vangie's interest in Seth surprised him. Especially after the question she'd asked him at the ranch.

"You don't need to be riding with us tonight, lad. We'll be circling their camp, looking for any sign they took the cattle. We've got more men than we need." Bram bent down, using both hands to cup water and splash it over his face. Straightening, he shook his head. "You should be going to town to see your lass."

Cam wanted nothing more than to see Vangie, make his interest clear, and spend a quiet evening alone with her. As always, he was torn between his own desires and responsibilities to his family.

He wondered how Fletcher had completed his duties at the ranch and still found time to court and marry Maddy. Their situation had been different in many other ways. Even though she was more of a town girl, they'd found a way to work out their differences. They had built a strong marriage and had a beautiful son.

Cam wanted what they had, what many of the MacLarens had already achieved. A woman he loved and who loved him, children, and a life surrounded by family. He startled, feeling Bram's hand on his shoulder.

"Listen to me, lad. No one will fault you for visiting your bonny lass tonight. We won't be making a decision about the gypsies until tomorrow."

Scrubbing both hands down his face, Cam's gaze moved over the corrals, barns, and four houses. He loved every inch of the ranch, every person who'd contributed to the success of Circle M. He'd never do anything to let them down.

"Go, lad. I'll let the others know." Bram squeezed his shoulder again before letting his hand drop to his side. "While you're there, be looking for a bonny lass for me."

Chapter Thirteen

Vangie stood in the middle of the parlor in her new home, taking a slow look around. Bay had been right. There were several beautiful, well-made pieces of furniture. Less than needed to fill the room, but enough for a start.

The dishes in the kitchen appeared to be almost new, as did the few pots on shelves next to the stove. Thankfully, the pantry had been cleaned out. No old cans of lard or jars of inedible fruit. One small table with two chairs had been placed in the middle of the room. She made a mental note to buy two more chairs, for no other reason than two didn't seem to be enough.

She'd already taken stock of the furniture in what would become her bedroom. The second bedroom was empty.

A soft knock on the front door didn't surprise her. Suzette had said she'd stop by before going to the restaurant. Opening the door, her breath caught at the sight of Cam, a cluster of wildflowers in his hand. He took a step toward her but didn't speak.

"Are those for me?"

Holding them out, he nodded. "Aye."

Taking them, she motioned for him to come inside before shutting the door. "These are lovely, Cam. Thanks so much."

He didn't respond, his attention on the house. "Suzette told me you bought this. You've decided to stay in Conviction then." Following her to the kitchen, a tightness grew in his chest. "You're happy in town, lass?"

Taking an empty jar from the cupboard, she filled it with water, placing the flowers inside. Setting it in the middle of the table, her attention focused on Cam. "I do like it in Conviction, and yes, I'm happy here. I've learned something about myself over the last few months."

Raising a brow, he cocked his head. "What would that be?"

"I can be happy almost anywhere, Cam. At first, I'd thought the move to another state would be difficult. It wasn't. I've learned it's about the people, being near those you care about."

"What about living on a ranch?"

The question caught her by surprise. She wondered at his reason for asking. "Why, yes, I do believe I could be happy on a ranch."

Cam relaxed only a little. Purchasing a house, moving from Bay and Suzette's created a set of problems he hadn't considered. Living with friends provided suitable chaperones for a single woman, lessening any talk of impropriety.

"It's a bonny house, lass."

"Thank you. Would you like to see the rest of it?"

He couldn't miss the joy in her voice, but knew it wouldn't be proper to see the bedrooms. Cam was about to tell her that when he heard a rap on the front door.

"That must be Suzette." Stepping past him, she hurried out of the kitchen to the door, pulling it open and motioning her friend inside. "I'm so glad you have time to come by. Cam just arrived." Vangie lowered her voice. "He brought me flowers."

"Good morning, Suzette."

"Hello, Cam. What do you think of Vangie's new home?"

He couldn't say what he felt. Cam wished she'd stayed with Suzette, but it wasn't his decision to make. "I don't like the lass being alone at night. Not with those men trying to find her."

Suzette shot Vangie a knowing look. "She's agreed to spend nights with us."

"For a while," Vangie said. "We don't even know if they're still searching for me. They may have given up and returned to Grand Rapids."

"Didn't Bay or Brodie tell you?" Suzette asked.

"Tell me what?"

"Brodie sent Seth to Sacramento. While he was there, he spotted a couple men he believes are the Riordan brothers. He didn't get their names, but they match the description Eustice gave us and traveled from back east. Seth plans to follow them to see if they're coming to Conviction."

Vangie frowned. "That's good news...isn't it?"

"Aye, lass, it is. We'll be able to protect you if we're knowing who they are." Cam was grateful Seth had spotted the men. It didn't mean he'd give up Vangie to him.

"What brought you to town today, Cam?" Suzette hoped it had been to invite Vangie to supper.

A small smile curved his mouth. "I'm here to invite Vangie to lunch." His gaze moved to her. "If you've no other plans, lass."

She worked to hide her excitement, knowing she'd failed at the smug look on Cam's face. "I'd love to have lunch with you."

Suzette looked between the two, hoping whatever came from his invitation would be good for both of them. She knew how Vangie felt about the tall, handsome rancher, and she was pretty certain Cam felt the same. He just needed a gentle push, which Seth provided.

"I'd better get to the restaurant. Will I see you there?"

"Aye. Unless there's somewhere else the lass wants to go." He glanced at Vangie.

"Feather River is perfect."

"Good. I'll see you two in a little while," Suzette said. "Lunch won't be served for another hour. Maybe Cam would like to see what you chose at Stein's warehouse."

Vangie's eyes lit up. "What a wonderful idea."

"Stein's warehouse?"

"You explain to Cam, Vangie. I need to get going."

Vangie waited until Suzette closed the door behind her before explaining. "Mr. Tharaldson has a warehouse at the docks where he stores furniture he's been given or bought from people who no longer need it. He sells the pieces at very good prices. I've already picked out several items."

"Seems you've been busy, lass."

She clasped her hands together, smiling. "Oh yes. Bay and Griff offered to move what I bought into the house tomorrow. It's all going to look wonderful."

"What time will they be at Stein's?"

"Eight o'clock."

"Then I'll be riding in to help, lass. Uncle Ewan says you can never have too much help."

Eyes going wide, her lips parted. "You don't have to do that, Cam. I know how busy you are at the ranch."

They were busy. Plus, he had to consider the missing cattle. Still, if Vangie needed help, he wanted to be there for her.

"No arguing, lass. I'll be riding in to help." He ignored the way her mouth tightened, preferring to change the subject. "Would you be ready for lunch?"

She let out a slow breath, shaking off his controlling personality. Vangie had to remind herself most strong men had a domineering streak. She didn't really want to be with a man who didn't. Many times, her father had said she needed a man as strong as her. Although he sometimes irritated her, Cam would fit the role. Vangie realized she wanted him to fit the role.

"Let me get my bonnet."

He spent the few minutes before she returned studying the parlor, dining room, and kitchen. Not wanting to like her new home, he tried to find fault with the size, the construction, anything to make him believe the house wasn't worthy of her.

By the time she joined him, Cam reluctantly admitted to himself the house fit her.

"I'm ready." Joining him, she noticed he'd stopped halfway between the kitchen and dining room, his face devoid of expression. "Is something wrong, Cam?"

Forcing his attention to her, he gave a quick shake of his head. "Nay, lass."

Touching her elbow, he guided her to the door. When outside, he held out his arm. Slipping hers through it, he couldn't help noticing how right she felt next to him. It took all his willpower not to bend down and kiss her cheek.

Cam promised himself by the end of the day, he'd be officially courting her.

Thane MacLaren worked his way through the thick brush, looking for a good position to watch the gypsy camp. He'd voiced his opinion about them going at night, but his uncles disagreed, believing they'd be able to see more in the daylight. The decision made watching the camp more difficult, more risky.

He'd joined Quinn, Colin, and Bram. An accomplishment, since none of the three wanted to place him in danger. Especially his oldest brothers, Quinn and Bram. Though he was almost seventeen, they still saw him as a child.

He'd hoped the decision allowing him to help his cousin, Blaine, at the ranch near Settlers Valley would've helped them see him as the young man he'd become. Instead, they were as protective as ever.

"Ach." The word burst from his lips at the noise from his boot breaking a fallen limb. Crouching, Thane looked around, hoping no one heard the sound.

The camp took up a good deal of space. Twelve wagons, over two dozen horses, and areas for cooking spread out over an acre of land, right on the edge of Circle M property.

Thane hunkered down between two boulders, setting his rifle next to him. His position was a good distance from the west edge of the camp. Not great for spotting evidence of slaughtered cattle.

He let out a disgusted oath, knowing this was already a waste of time. They should've approached after dark when they could get closer, have a better view of the camp. Maybe even watch as they cooked a fresh slab of beef.

Drawing his revolver from its holster, he checked the cylinder. Nothing had changed since the last time he made certain each chamber held a bullet. Slipping the six-shooter away, he shifted to a more comfortable position, frustrated at his inability to get a good view of the camp. He needed to be at least twenty yards closer, which could happen once the sun set.

The four had left their horses a good distance from each of their locations. Far enough away so the occupants of the camp couldn't hear them. Close enough to reach them in a hurry.

The sound of crunching leaves caught his attention. Thane twisted to look behind him, seeing nothing. Several minutes of silence followed. He wanted to stand and look around, but didn't dare take the chance.

Frustration overwhelmed him. He hated wasting time doing a job he knew would show no results while his chores piled up. Everyone on the ranch had been putting in more time than usual. They needed to hire more men, a job falling to Ewan and Ian.

Peeking around the boulder, he looked through the trees, seeing people move within the camp. Some carried wood, others stood around talking, while a few worked on strands of rope or leather. What he couldn't see from this distance was any sign of slaughtered cattle, and knew Quinn, Bram, or Colin wouldn't be able to see anything, either.

Again, the sound of crunching leaves had him turning, his body stilling. A man stood in the trees, a gun in his hand. Thane didn't have time to grab his rifle or draw his revolver before a shot rang out. A sharp pain pierced his chest.

Fighting for consciousness, he fumbled for the butt of his gun as his body slumped down. A moment later, his eyes closed on a deep, guttural groan.

Chapter Fourteen

Conviction

Cam didn't want to return to the ranch. Lunch with Vangie had been wonderful. Better than expected, which shouldn't have surprised him. They'd gotten along well from the first day they'd met under less than desirable circumstances, both waiting on news about Suzette's safety.

He'd sat next to her at Bay and Suzette's wedding celebration and seen her a few times since, enjoying every encounter. Then his reservations about their divergent backgrounds began to weigh on him.

Cam was a rancher through and through. She'd never lived outside the confines of a town, enjoying the amenities not found on a ranch. Vangie didn't understand the long hours, endless chores, and small amounts of sleep common for those who chose the life of a rancher. In fact, she'd never worked a day in her life.

From their short conversations, her days back home involved shopping, needlepoint, reading, and social engagements. He knew she volunteered at the Home for Displaced Children, and she hoped to help homeless children in Conviction. Which caused a problem, as there wasn't a home for orphans. Those few found homes with ranchers or those living in town. It didn't mean a need wouldn't arise at some point, but for now, the children were absorbed into existing families.

Before lunch, he'd accompanied her to Stein's, amused at her enthusiasm over the few pieces of furniture she'd purchased. After their meal, he'd escorted her around town, looking into shop windows, talking of what else she needed at her new place. Vangie agreed there wasn't much she required. There were many items she *wanted*.

They'd made it back to her house late afternoon, drinking coffee while they spoke of him growing up farming, then ranching when the MacLarens moved to Conviction. She told Cam about life in Grand Rapids, her friendship with Eustice, and the loss of her parents.

It was something they had in common. He'd lost his father and Uncle Gillis. Cam wished they had more shared experiences than losing those they loved.

Setting down his empty cup, he glanced through the windows, knowing he'd already spent hours in her company. It didn't mean he wanted to let her go just yet, and not before he'd voiced his intentions to court her.

"If you've no plans, would you have supper with me, lass?"

A tentative smile curved her lips. "I'd think you would be tired of me by now, Cam."

"You would be wrong, Vangie."

A slight blush crept up her face, enhancing her bright, blue eyes. Glancing down into her lap, she cleared her throat. "Then I'd love to have supper with you, Cam."

Standing, he held out his hand, then stilled at an insistent pounding on her front door. Closing the distance to the door, he pulled it open, stunned to see Bram, unable to miss the anxiety on his cousin's face.

"What's wrong, lad?"

"It's Thane. He's been shot."

Hearing the conversation, Vangie joined them. "How bad is he?"

"We've taken him to the clinic." Bram sucked in a breath. "It's bad."

Grabbing his gunbelt from a hook by the door, Cam fastened it around his hips before snatching his hat. Facing Vangie, he opened his mouth to speak before she cut off his words.

"I'm coming with you." Rushing to a nearby table, she retrieved her bonnet, reticule, and shawl before hurrying back. "Shall we go?"

Grabbing her shoulders, Cam searched her face. "You don't have to go, lass. There won't be much any of us can do but wait."

"Then I'll wait with you. We're wasting time, Cam." Stepping past him, she dashed to the street, heading straight to the clinic.

"What happened?" Cam asked Bram.

"We were watching the gypsy camp when we heard a shot. By the time Colin, Quinn, and I found Thane, the shooter was gone and the lad was surrounded by the gypsies. They were yelling at him but doing nothing to help."

Reaching the clinic, Cam swung the door open, letting Vangie and Bram in ahead of him. Inside, Quinn and Colin paced, their faces set in stone.

Bram moved to Quinn. "How is he?"

"We don't know. Doc Vickery is taking care of the lad." Scrubbing a hand down his face, Quinn stared at the floor. "Thane shouldn't have been with us."

"Did you send word to Ma?" Bram asked.

Giving a quick shake of his head, Quinn shot a look at Colin. "Nae. We've not told Brodie, either."

"I'll go." Cam took Vangie's elbow, guiding her back to the door and outside.

Without speaking, they crossed the street, dodging wagons and riders on their way to the jail. Stepping onto the boardwalk, Cam shoved the door open, spotting Sam.

"Where's Brodie?"

Pushing out of the chair, Sam's gaze moved from Cam to Vangie, unable to miss their troubled expressions. "He rode out to the Belford ranch with Alex. Why?"

"Thane's been shot."

Grabbing his hat, Sam started for the door. "I need to let Jinny know. Where is he, Cam?"

"Doc Vickery is tending him. Get Jinny and meet us back there." Sam's wife, Jinny, was Brodie's sister. "She'll be wanting to be with him."

"Does his ma know?" Sam asked as he headed outside.

"Nae, she doesn't."

"Should I send Jack to tell her? He's the only deputy left in town."

Vangie gripped Cam's arm before he could answer. "Jack should stay here. I'll go for her."

Cupping her face in his hands, he shook his head. "Nae, lass. You cannot be going alone."

"I'll get Eustice—"

"And Bay," Cam interjected. "We don't know who shot the lad or where he is."

Turning her face, she kissed the palm of his hand. Another bold move she doubted he'd approve. "All right."

Feeling a shiver run through him at the feel of her lips, he bent down, placing a kiss on her forehead. "Don't bother with a wagon. Ride straight to Circle M and get Aunt Audrey. Ask any of the lads to saddle her horse. It will be faster than a wagon."

"I'll bring her back, Cam. You keep watch on Thane."

Moving past Sam and out the door, she picked up her skirts and ran to the livery, ignoring the curious looks of those she passed. "Eustice! Eustice, where are you?"

Hurrying through the blacksmith shop, she entered the livery, her anxious gaze darting around.

"What is it, Vangie?" Wiping his hands on a rag, he emerged from a nearby stall, walking toward her.

"I need you to saddle horses for you, Bay, and me."

Cocking his head, his brows scrunched together. "Why?"

"Thane MacLaren has been shot. We need to ride to Circle M to get his mother."

Eyes wide, he dropped the rag on the ground. "I can do that, Vangie."

"Wonderful, Eustice. I'll find Bay."

"Don't worry, Vangie. I'll be ready with the horses."

"You cannot stay here, Jean-Paul." Anger and fear tinged Belcher's words, agitation clear in the way he paced in front of the fire.

Staring at the man who'd been his friend their entire lives, Jean-Paul spread his arms out. "This is my home. I've got nowhere else to go."

"You shot a boy. A *boy*!"

"But he was watching the camp, spying on us."

Shoving hands through his hair, Belcher's face turned a deep purple, eyes bulging. "He couldn't have seen anything from where you found him. If he dies, the entire town will come down on us."

"They don't know who shot him."

"And they won't find out if you leave, Jean-Paul. We won't be able to protect you if they learn you're the one who shot the boy."

Snorting, he crossed his arms. "He was not a boy."

"Those of us who saw him believe differently. You must leave us. You've no wife or children to consider. I have the entire family to think about. Your foolish actions have put all of us in danger."

"If I leave, who will protect the family? Certainly not you, Belcher. You don't have the stomach for what I have to do. Who will find food? A few men hunt, but not well. They steal, but aren't capable of providing the way I do." Taking purposeful steps, he stopped inches from Belcher. "You are angry with what I did, but it was to protect all of us. We cannot have outsiders spying on us, Belcher. You *know* that is true."

Not backing away but lowering his voice, he pinned Jean-Paul with a hard glare. "You are too quick to kill. No matter how much we depend on you, you've blackness in your heart. A blackness that puts us all in peril."

"You cannot ban me without a vote, Belcher."

As much as he wanted to argue, Jean-Paul was right. Forcing someone from the family took a majority vote, not an order from their leader. One

135

other time he'd called a vote on Jean-Paul for a similar offense. He'd been outvoted. Belcher suspected the same would happen this time, and Jean-Paul knew it.

"You cannot be here if they come to search our camp."

"Then let me search for food and scout places where we may live without fear of being turned away."

Shaking his head, Belcher gave a mirthless chuckle. "There is no such place, Jean-Paul. We've traveled since I was a boy, and there is never a place for us."

"Because we refuse to live by their laws, doing the type of work they find suitable. They don't respect our customs. They laugh at our ways. They come to us when they want to be entertained or have their fortune told. Behind our backs, they ridicule us, Belcher."

"If you believe there's no place for us anywhere, where do you intend we go?"

"I've heard there are places up north where people such as us are welcome."

"How far north, Jean-Paul?"

"Outside of Portland in the state of Oregon."

Glancing around the camp, Belcher thought of the women and children, and the upcoming winter. "That is hundreds of miles away."

"Far away from Conviction and the trouble you believe I've brought upon us."

"Leaving will solve nothing if you do not change your ways, Jean-Paul. You cannot kill without reason. That boy was no harm to us, yet you shot him. If he dies, we'll have no choice but to turn you over."

"We do not turn over our people to outsiders."

"No, but a murder has never occurred near where we camp. What you've done is not something we can shield you from. If the boy dies and they come here, you will have to leave."

Chapter Fifteen

Reggie stuck his head out the stagecoach window into the early morning sun, quickly pulling it back. The spiraling dust coated his clothing, clogged his throat, and stung his eyes.

"I cannot wait until we reach our next stop and get back on solid ground." Swiping his hands over his clothing did nothing but stir more dust into the air. "We should've stayed longer in Sacramento. At least it was more civilized than most small towns we've been through."

Merle put a handkerchief to his mouth, choking on the dust and his brother's inane comment. "You're the one determined to find the woman and retrieve our money. I would've been content to stay home and move on to other ventures."

"The funds Miss Rousseau owes us is worth *ten* new ventures."

Finding it difficult to draw in a breath, Merle choked, spitting out the stage's open window. "I doubt the lady will simply hand over the money because we ask."

A shrewd gleam shown in Reggie's eyes. "Then we must persuade her."

"We've spoken of this before. I'll not be a party to you hurting a woman."

Putting a hand over his heart, he feigned offense. "I can't believe you'd think I would hurt her. I'm a man of peace, Merle."

If his throat hadn't been clogged with dust, he would've laughed at his brother's ridiculous statement. "You guarantee you'll not lay a hand on her?"

"We'll use persuasion, Merle, not force." The jostling of the wagon forced him back against the seat. "The roads out west are far worse than those back home."

"Why would you expect them to be better? Nothing out here is anything like we have back home. We never should've left on this merciless journey."

"If Rousseau and his wife hadn't died, we wouldn't have been forced to follow their daughter."

"If you hadn't hired men to tamper with his wagon, he'd still be alive and we could've gotten our money from him."

"They were supposed to scare Rousseau, not cause him to topple into a ravine when the axle broke. The men were incompetent."

"You were the one to hire them, Reggie. And you did it on your own. I wouldn't have agreed to such foolishness."

"I did what I thought best. If you recall, you were busy with your mistress. Something had to be done or he would've taken our money and vanished."

Merle braced himself as the stage moved over an especially brutal stretch of road. "He never said anything about leaving town, Reggie. You were the one who thought he planned to cheat us. I never believed that was the case. We're lucky no one traced their deaths back to us."

Keeping one hand clutched on the edge of the seat, he waved the other in the air. "It no longer matters. We find Evangeline Rousseau, persuade her to return our funds, and go home."

Glancing at him, Merle did what had become his way of dealing with the burning knot of worry in his gut. He ignored it.

Conviction

Vangie woke on a yawn, feeling a strong arm tighten around her shoulders. Eyes opening to slits, she stared at the fabric of a man's shirt, felt her head nestled against hard muscle. Shifting, she lifted her head, staring into golden brown eyes.

"Good morning, lass."

Blinking, she sat up, looking at the others waiting for word on Thane. Vangie wiped sleep from her eyes, then smoothed hands over her wrinkled shirt, already missing the solid warmth of Cam's chest.

"Have you heard anything?"

"Nae, lass. Doc Vickery came out twice to tell us the lad hasn't woken up. He did say there's no fever."

She set her hand on his arm, squeezing. "That's very good news. How's his mother doing?"

Stretching his arms over his head, Cam looked at Audrey. She sat between her son, Quinn, and nephew, Colin. All wore stoic expressions.

"She waits for word the same as the rest of us."

Vangie stared across the room, wishing she knew what to say. The trip back from Circle M the evening before had been quiet, Audrey riding her horse with squared shoulders. Bay had flanked her while Eustice and Vangie rode behind.

Audrey had said less than a dozen words after arriving at the clinic and asking about Thane's condition. When learning there was no news, she'd fallen silent.

Vangie's heart went out to the older woman. She understood sorrow, the loss of her parents cutting deep and changing her life. The woman had already lost her husband. Losing a child was more than Vangie could imagine.

"I should visit Suzette, ask her to have breakfast delivered." Starting to rise, she stopped when Cam's hand grasped her wrist.

"Bay has already taken care of it, lass. Sit with me a little longer. Or, if you wish, I'll escort you back home."

Covering his hand with hers, she relaxed back against the chair. "I'd be happy to stay as long as you need me, Cam."

Leaning closer, he lowered his voice. "When this is over, lass, I'll be asking to court you. Will you be giving me the answer I want, Miss Rousseau?"

A small smile tilted her lips. "Yes. I do believe you'll get the answer you want, Mr. MacLaren."

Cam wanted to kiss her, but didn't dare. Not with his brother, cousins, and aunt in the room.

The door to Thane's room opened, Doc Vickery walking out. Everyone stood, taking slow steps toward him. A tight smile formed on the doctor's face.

"Thane is drifting in and out of consciousness, but there's still no fever, which is an excellent sign. A few inches to the right and there would've been nothing I could do. As it is, if he gets through the next forty-eight hours, he should recover."

Audrey placed a hand over her mouth, covering a quiet sob as Quinn's arm went around her.

"May Ma see him, Doctor?"

"Yes, for a few minutes, Quinn." Motioning for Audrey to follow, Vickery held the door open, allowing Quinn to take a look inside before closing the door.

"So this is Conviction. Not much different from Sacramento, except smaller." Jeffrey Tipton stepped from the stage, moving a slow circle before looking at his younger brother, Wayne. "A boardinghouse, a couple of hotels on the main street. At least we'll have our choice of places to stay."

Setting down the bag the driver tossed to him, Wayne's gaze latched onto the sign for the Gold Dust Hotel and Restaurant. "I'd prefer a hotel. With luck, we'll complete our business and be on our way home in a few days."

Gripping his bag, Jeffrey continued to scan the street before nodding. "My thoughts also."

Focusing on the men and women they passed, both made their way along the boardwalk. "Do you still have the address for our meeting?"

Setting his bag next to Wayne's, Jeffrey reached into his pocket, withdrawing a paper with the address. Handing it to his brother, he glanced down the street at the jail. "I'm certain it won't take long to locate it. Let's find a room and clean up. Tomorrow, we can walk around town and make inquiries."

Making a slow circle, Wayne stood with his hands on his hips. "Perhaps this town isn't as small as I first thought. Not as big as Sacramento, but still more suitable for our business than I imagined."

Picking up his bag, he glanced around, failing to notice the man riding down the middle of the street. If he had, Jeffrey would've recognized him as the one who'd introduced himself to them in Sacramento. He might have even been curious as to what brought him to Conviction or why he'd dismounted in front of the jail and walked inside. But he saw none of this.

Instead, he nodded up the street. "Let's find a place to stay and walk around before supper."

They passed a couple hotels, saloons, and other shops before circling back to enter the Gold Dust. Neither noticed the deputy watching them from across the street.

If they had, they wouldn't have been smiling when they approached the registration counter.

Chapter Sixteen

"What will you be doing about it, Brodie?" Quinn tried not to let his anger show. His cousin was a competent sheriff. The best man who'd ever held the position in Conviction. Still, he'd done little since learning of Thane being shot.

Resting his arms on the top of his desk, he leaned forward. "Until the lad's able to talk, tell me what he saw, there's little I can do."

"We know the gypsies did it, Brodie." Colin stared out the front window of the jail, trying to calm the worry he felt.

"Aye, but which one? We can't be charging all of them. Alex and Sam rode out to the spot where Thane was shot and found nothing. No blood. Nothing."

"Ach. You know those miscreants cleaned it up." Pacing to the stove, Quinn poured a cup of coffee, wincing at the bitter taste.

"We should be riding in as a group, scare them into talking," Colin tossed over his shoulder at Brodie, not turning from the window.

"Gypsies don't turn in their own. We'll not be getting even one to talk."

Walking to the back door, Quinn tossed the last of his coffee outside. "Aye. But if we get one alone, we would have a chance."

Turning away from the window, one corner of Colin's mouth curved upward. "We can do that, lad. We've the men and are a short distance from their camp. They have to be leaving for town sometime."

"And one of our lads will be there," Quinn added.

Clearing his throat loud enough to gain their attention, Brodie crossed his arms over his wide chest. "You'll not be doing anything causing me to arrest you."

"We'll not be hurting anyone," Quinn said.

Brodie narrowed his gaze on him. "You'd best not."

"Whoever we find, we'll bring them to you to question. Fair enough?" Colin quirked a brow, waiting for a response from a man as close to him as his brothers.

Steepling his fingers under his chin, Brodie considered his cousins' proposal. They weren't lawmen, which meant the gypsies would be less on guard. Certainly less than if Brodie or one of his deputies rode in.

"I'll have your promise no one will be hurt."

"Aye," Colin said at once.

"Aye." Quinn grinned. "Not a hair, lad."

The door opening caught their attention. "Seth. I've been wondering when you'd return." Brodie stood, motioning to Colin and Quinn. "I'd like you to stay here while we go to the clinic."

Tossing his hat on a chair, Seth shot a concerned look at Brodie. "Is someone hurt?"

Grabbing his own hat, Brodie nodded. "Aye. Thane was shot near the gypsy camp. It's been almost two days and the lad has yet to wake up enough to talk."

"Damn, Brodie. I didn't know. You believe it was one of the gypsies?" Seth asked.

"Aye, and I mean to find out which one."

Cam slipped Vangie's arm through his. It was close to noon, and Thane still hadn't woken. Suzette had brought breakfast for those in the waiting room, but Cam needed air, and time alone with Vangie.

The amazement of her accepting his request to court her hadn't lessened. The more he thought about it, the more he realized how right his decision had been. She was strong, resilient, and willing to live on the ranch. Cam felt certain she'd take it with the ease she accepted everything else. No matter she'd never worked. She had helped run a household, knew what was required to succeed.

The courtship would give them both time to be certain of their feelings. He wanted to take her to Circle M for several days, have her spend time with his family. She could stay with one of his aunts, help with meals, and participate in the daily chores required on a ranch.

None of it would happen until Thane recovered and they'd found the man responsible for shooting him.

"He will wake up, Cam. I'm certain of it." Vangie placed her hand over his, offering a warm smile. "Thane will recover and be back working cattle before you know it."

Ignoring the ball of worry clogging his throat, Cam drew her closer as they crossed the street, approaching the Great West Café. "Aye, lass. The lad will make it. Of that I'm sure."

"When he does, do you think I might spend time at your ranch?" Wincing at another bold, quite inappropriate question, she looked away. "I apologize, Cam. It was an unsuitable request."

Halting a few feet from the café, he settled his hands on her shoulders, turning her to him. A glint of humor shown in his caramel brown eyes before his lips twitched, head thrown back on a deep laugh.

"Ah, lass. You continue to surprise me." Letting his hands slip down her arms, he took her hands in his. "You're welcome at the ranch anytime, Vangie."

He couldn't believe she'd broached the subject before him. It was as if she could read his mind. Brushing a finger down her cheek, a possessive gleam showed in his eyes.

"We'll be having a fine time of it, lass. A bonny fine time."

Seth stood with his back against the outside wall of the jail, struggling with what he saw. He'd watched as Cam and Vangie walked on the other side of the street, neither noticing him. His trip to Sacramento had been necessary, but the timing hadn't worked in his favor.

Thinking back, Seth knew he should've spoken of his interest in Vangie sooner, asked permission to court her. Instead, he'd assumed there'd be time, ignoring what he believed to be her interest in Cam.

If he were being honest, seeing them together wasn't a surprise. As much as he liked Vangie, seeing her with Cam didn't bother him as much as it should. The same as all the MacLarens, Seth liked and respected him, considered Cam a friend.

Staring down at his boots, he shook his head, a small smile curving his lips. He never had a chance with Vangie. Still, he'd enjoyed every minute in her company.

Glancing up, Seth pushed from the wall, observing one of the two men he'd seen in Sacramento exit the hotel. He'd followed them to Conviction, certain they were the men Eustice spoke about.

After watching them check into the hotel, Seth had hurried to the jail, letting Brodie know of their whereabouts. Now he kept watch, spotting one brother stroll along the boardwalk.

Seth had already spent time with an older man who often registered guests at the Gold Dust. Giving descriptions, he'd been told no one named Riordan had taken a room. But they did have two men named Tipton. Seth would bet his last penny they were the Riordan brothers but had decided to register under assumed names. Given the nefarious reason for their visit to Conviction, Seth wasn't surprised.

Not wanting Tipton to know he approached, Seth kept his gaze moving over the street and boardwalk as he followed. They made a circle of the main street, then walked to the block behind, passing the newspaper office, Feather River Hotel, millinery and dress shop, a smaller hotel, and a saloon before circling back to the Gold Dust.

Tipton didn't act like someone who had anything to hide. His relaxed manner, unconcern for anyone following, confused Seth. He'd expected the brothers to ask questions of local merchants and the sheriff. Tipton made no move to enter any of the shops or speak with the townsfolk while making his stroll around town.

Once back on the main street, he didn't walk toward the hotel. Continuing the slow pace, he stopped for several moments in front of the law offices of Fielder, Donahue, and MacKenzie.

Pausing twenty feet away, Seth looked into the gunsmith shop while sending careful glances at the man every few seconds. After a couple minutes, he shifted his stance when Tipton opened the door and disappeared into the building, leaving Seth to wonder what business he might have with August, Bay, or Griff.

Continuing his vigil, he sat down on a bench outside the gunsmith shop, stretching out his long legs. From this location, he could see almost all the businesses on the main street. The ones of most interest were the hotel and law offices.

Leaning forward, he pulled up his legs, resting his arms on his thighs. The shift almost caused him to miss the other Tipton brother exiting the hotel. Standing, Seth turned away as the man crossed the street to enter the law offices.

Confusion mounting, Seth stood for several moments, deciding it best to wait until the brothers left their meeting. He needed to speak with August or Bay, learn the reason for their visit.

Sitting back down on the bench, he again stretched out his legs, stilling. Across the street, two men emerged from the hotel. Both identical in size and dress as the brothers he'd been watching.

"Mrs. MacLaren?" Jonathon Vickery stepped from the examination room.

"Yes, Doctor?" Audrey straightened, her features strained, showing the toll her son's injury had exacted on her. Red-rimmed eyes, pinched expression, and drawn lines at her mouth showed the extent of her worry.

"Thane is awake." Scrambling to their feet, Quinn and Bram helped their mother up. "Only Mrs. MacLaren for now." Vickery pulled the door wide. "I'm sorry, but you can stay but a few minutes."

"As long as you'll allow me."

Leaving the door open enough for Quinn and Bram to look in, Vickery moved to the opposite side of the bed. One glance at her son, and Audrey hurried forward. Seeing his eyes closed, she brushed strands of hair from his face and leaned down.

"Thane, lad. Can you hear me?" She watched as his eyes opened to slits, a hint of recognition in them.

"Ma?"

A relieved smile spread across her face, even as she worked to block the tears. "Aye, lad."

Blinking slowly, Thane licked his lips. "Is there water, Ma?"

Handing her a glass, Vickery helped her hold his head up enough to drink. "Just a little for now, Thane," he said, taking the glass from Audrey's hand.

Thane's blurred gaze tried to focus on his mother. "What happened?"

"You were shot."

Closing his eyes, Thane's brows bunched together. "Shot?"

"Aye. You were watching the gypsy camp when someone shot you."

"Gypsy camp..." His words trailed off as Thane drifted back to sleep.

Skimming fingers down his cheek, Audrey allowed one tear to escape. "Sleep, my boy. Sleep and heal." She looked at Vickery. "Is Thane out of danger?"

Removing the spectacles he'd begun to wear, Vickery took a moment before answering. "If there's no infection, he should be strong enough to return home in a few days, although he won't be ready to start work for a couple weeks."

Pursing her lips, Audrey nodded, relief easing the lines on her face. "Thank you."

"It's Thane's doing, not mine. He's strong and young. I believe he'll come through this, but it will take time."

"Can I be sitting with him a while?"

"As long as you let him sleep."

Lowering herself into a chair, she took Thane's hand in hers. Lowering her head, she began to pray.

Chapter Seventeen

Cam watched Bram work the colt, his mind drifting to Vangie. He hadn't seen her for three days. Not since they'd been told Thane could return to the ranch. So far, he hadn't been able to remember anything about the person who'd shot him.

After speaking with Brodie and Seth about the men they were following, he hadn't wanted to leave Vangie alone in town. His cousin had assured him deputies, as well as Eustice, would be watching her day and night, allowing no one to get near. Bay's promise she'd be staying with him and Suzette until they figured out who was after her gave him little peace. Neither did Bay's assertion the two men he and August had met with had no interest in Vangie.

Cam should be the man protecting her. Thane being shot had stalled work at the ranch, and Army contracts to provide horses loomed ahead.

Unfortunately, Brodie had come no closer to identifying the man responsible for shooting Thane. Until he regained his memory, they had nothing to go on, not a single idea about who fired the shot.

"Why don't you ride to town and see your lass?"

So lost in his thoughts, Cam hadn't noticed Bram had finished with the colt, putting the animal away before joining him at the fence. "Nae, I'm needed here."

"We've got Thane back home."

"Still means you're short a man."

Bram clasped his cousin's shoulder. "We've been short men before. The uncles left for town early this morning to hire more. You're free to go to your lass."

A slow grin slid the corners of Cam's mouth upward. "Aye. Perhaps I *will* be riding to town this afternoon. Not before we finish with the colts."

"Then we'd best not be dallying, lad." Heading behind the barn to the pens holding the colts, Bram brought two out, handing one over to Cam. "You should be bringing the lass here, Cam."

"Aye, I plan to after Thane remembers enough to describe the man who shot him."

"Doc Vickery said he might never be recalling the events of that day. If you're worried about the ride from town with the lass, I'll go with you."

Cam was tempted to accept Bram's offer. Keeping Vangie safe while believing one of the two sets of men were after her kept him up at night. He'd not slept more than a few hours since learning Seth's news. Even with Brodie's men watching the four, escorting Vangie to Circle M presented a risk.

"Aye, it's an excellent idea, Bram. You'll be riding into town with me this afternoon. You'll have supper with us at the Feather River."

Turning his attention from the colt to Cam, he thought of all they had to accomplish before leaving. "What if the lass has plans?"

A brash smile appeared. "She won't."

Conviction

"None of the four have asked about Vangie or visited Eustice. In fact, they've stayed well away from the livery." Seth tossed his hat on Brodie's desk in disgust. "Bay is certain we should concentrate on the two who aren't his clients."

"Maybe the lad's right. He sent telegrams to New York. They're from a well-known family. Their father sent them west to invest in properties, which is why they met with Bay and August."

Massaging the back of his neck, Seth nodded his understanding. "I trust his judgment. It's just..." His voice trailed off when the door opened. Cam walked in, followed by Bram.

Standing, Brodie pulled each of his cousins into a hug. "What brings you lads to town?" Stepping away, he studied Cam's face. "Ach, it's the lass."

"How is she?"

"Vangie's fine, Cam. Alex is watching her." Sitting back down, Brodie motioned for them to do the same before nodding at Seth. "Bay heard from his contacts. The brothers are legitimate."

"Their father sent them here to talk with Bay and August about investing in land," Seth added. "Bay says they've already made offers on a large plot."

"We'll be concentrating on the other two lads," Brodie said. "We've not been able to determine why they're in town."

"Have you talked to them?" Bram asked.

"Nae. We've been following. So far, they've done nothing suspicious. Seth spoke with bartenders, Mr. Maloney at the mercantile, and workers in the restaurants. The lads have been friendly, asked about the town and the docks. They haven't asked about Vangie."

Cam looked out the window, the information not comforting him the way he'd hoped. He didn't turn around. "Maybe none of them are the men after her."

Seth shifted in the chair to look at Cam. "We've seen no one else matching the description Eustice gave us."

"Perhaps they've not arrived," Bram said.

Brodie folded his hands on the desk. "Then we will have to continue watching for anyone coming into Conviction we don't know. We'll not be letting anything happen to your lass, Cam."

He didn't consider arguing over his cousin's comment. Vangie was his, and he planned to make sure everyone knew it. "Bram and I will be off to find her. We'll be taking her to supper at the Feather River."

"Then be off with you and let us do our work." Brodie's dismissal was accompanied by a broad smile.

Stepping outside, Cam stopped long enough to scan the street. He'd been so certain either the Tiptons or the other two men were those after Vangie, he'd begun to relax, if only a little. It now seemed none of them were the men they sought.

"Brodie will make sure no one gets near the lass, Cam. You need to be trusting him." Bram stood next to him, his gaze also wandering over the town.

"Aye, you're right."

"You can stay in town if you feel the need to watch her yourself."

Cam shifted his feet, considering it before shaking his head. "Nae. I've work at the ranch that we can't be putting off any longer. Taking this evening off to spend with Vangie is as much as I can do now. Come on. Let's go find the lass."

"This was a wonderful idea, Suzette. I'm so tired of staying inside, afraid the men may have already arrived." Vangie looked inside the mercantile window, her attention latching onto a new parasol. Another item she found fetching but didn't need.

"It's my day off and I mean to make the most of it. As you know, I spend most days off cleaning and picking up provisions at the mercantile. Rarely do I spend time shopping for fun. There's simply no time for it."

"Well, today there is. Shall we finish with the millinery before having an early supper? My treat, Suzette."

"I can't let you pay for my supper, Vangie."

"Of course you can."

Stopping outside the millinery and dress shop, her gaze moved down the boardwalk to the small hotel at the end of the block. "Have you been inside the Boundary Hotel?"

Suzette followed Vangie's gaze. "Why, yes. It's quite lovely. Small with about a dozen rooms, but they're very nice. Linens from Europe and statues brought all the way from Rome. Breakfast is included, as is high tea and wine in the afternoons. Bay says it's owned by a financier from San Francisco. He bought it from the original owner not long ago."

"It must be quite expensive."

"More than the Feather River. Truthfully, it would be the perfect place for newlyweds or visitors looking for more intimacy." A glint of mischief showed in Suzette's eyes. "I'd like to take Bay there one night. Just to experience it, of course."

Vangie bit back a grin. "Research?"

"Exactly. I just need to pick a time when we won't be interrupted." Opening the door of the millinery, they stepped over the threshold.

"Oh my. Mrs. Abbott has added so many new dresses and hats since I was last inside." Vangie moved to a display when the owner entered from the back.

"Mrs. Donahue, Miss Rousseau, what an unexpected surprise."

Suzette offered her a warm smile. "It's been much too long since I've been here. How is your son?"

"Quite well. Conviction is so much better for us than Sacramento."

Cynthia Abbott had moved to town after the unexpected death of her husband. A single mother of twenty-two, she'd had the courage to use the money her late husband left to take a chance on opening a store in Conviction. Suzette had hired Cynthia to create her wedding dress.

"You've added so much. The shop is truly beautiful."

"Thank you, Miss Rousseau. It's taken a while, but I am quite pleased with the results. Is there something I may help you ladies find?"

"I'd appreciate your help selecting a dress," Vangie replied.

"Is it for a special occasion?" Cynthia walked to a wall showcasing her newest creations.

Shooting a quick look at Suzette, she did her best to hide the thrill still coursing through her at Cam's request to court her. "There is. Camden MacLaren has asked to court me and I've accepted."

Unable to hide her surprise, Suzette's eyes flashed. "What? When did this happen and why haven't you told me before now?"

"I haven't had a chance to say anything."

Crossing her arms, Suzette glared at her. "I will not accept that excuse, Vangie. You're living with Bay and me for a little longer, and we see each other several times a day. So, tell me the real reason you've kept the news from me."

"Perhaps I should give the two of you some privacy."

Holding up a hand, Vangie stopped Cynthia from leaving. "Please stay." She looked at Suzette. "The reason I haven't said anything is because I've been afraid he'll change his mind. Silly, I know. But..." Shrugging, she sent her closest friend a pleading gaze.

"Oh, Vangie. Cam would never change his mind about something as important as a courtship. To be truthful, I expected him to ask you weeks ago."

A blush crept up Vangie's face as she looked between the two women. "Well, I do believe he wasn't pleased with me sharing meals with Deputy Montero."

"Regardless of the reason, I'm so happy he offered. He's so perfect for you, Vangie."

"Well, yes, I do believe he is. I just don't want to disappoint him."

Setting her hands on Vangie's shoulders, Suzette squeezed. "How could you possibly disappoint him?"

She stared at the floor, the blush deepening. "He wants a ranch wife."

Dropping her hands, Suzette lifted a brow. "And?"

"Don't be dull, Suzette. We both know I have no experience on a ranch."

"You can ride, cook, and clean. What more is there to know?"

"That's just it. I know there must be more."

"Cam is a wonderful man. All you have to do is ask him what he expects. You're a very clever woman, Vangie. What you don't know you'll learn."

Sucking in a slow breath, she pursed her lips, praying her friend was right.

Chapter Eighteen

Cam knocked again on Vangie's door, getting no response. Turning around, he scanned the street looking for Alex, the deputy Brodie assigned to guard her.

"Perhaps the lass is at Bay and Suzette's." Bounding down the steps, Cam walked to the end of the block, mounting the steps to their front door. Knocking, he stepped back and waited, tension knotting the muscles in his shoulders.

"Let's try the restaurant, lad. Vangie may be there with Suzette." Bram headed down the steps.

The back of the Feather River Hotel and Restaurant faced the street where Vangie, Bay, and Suzette lived. Entering the back door, they made their way through a short hallway, hearing the sounds of people working in the kitchen.

Emerging into the large dining room, their attention turned to Suzette's assistant, Zeke Clayton. He stood with a small group of servers, preparing for the supper service.

The hotel and restaurant had been built by August Fielder, Bay Donahue, and the MacLaren family. Patterned after premier establishments back east, it offered the finest fare in the region. It wasn't unusual for residents of the San Francisco Bay area and Sacramento to travel to Conviction, securing rooms in the hotel and eating in the first class restaurant.

Finishing, Zeke spotted them. "Cam, Bram. It's good to see you." Shaking their hands, he nodded toward the tables. "We aren't open for supper yet, but you're welcome to sit down and have a drink."

"Thank you, but we're trying to find Vangie. Has she been here today?"

"No, Cam. I haven't seen her in a couple days."

"What about Suzette?" Bram asked.

"It's her day off. Have you checked both houses?"

"Aye. No one answered the door," Cam answered.

Rubbing his brow, Zeke stared out the front window a moment before returning his attention to Cam and Bram.

"A couple days ago, Suzette mentioned wanting to do some shopping. Vangie often goes with her. Have you checked the mercantile, millinery, and other shops?"

"Not yet, but we'll be doing that now. Thank you, Zeke."

"I hope you find the ladies, Cam. If they come here, I'll send someone to find you."

"It's perfect, Mrs. Abbott." Vangie stroked her hands down the split riding skirt Cynthia had made for another woman. The customer had never returned or paid for the beautiful clothing, making it available to someone else.

"If you'd like to see it, there's a blouse I created to go with the skirt."

"Yes, I would."

Suzette moved closer, admiring the design. "It fits as if it had been made for you, Vangie. If the blouse is as wonderful as I suspect, you'll have to buy both."

"Here it is." Cynthia held out the finely made item. "Would you like try it on?"

"Please." Disappearing behind a curtain, she emerged a minute later. "What do you think?" She made a slow turn, giving them a good look at the outfit.

"I thought it would fit you, Miss Rousseau. There's nothing I need to adjust."

"Mrs. Abbott is right, Vangie. All you need now is a coat." Suzette's brow lifted a fraction at Cynthia.

"I do believe there's a coat that will fill the need." Hurrying to the back, she came out seconds later, a wool coat draped over one arm. "This should work well for you, Miss Rousseau."

Slipping it on, Vangie checked the sleeves and length. "I do believe I'll take all three items."

Cynthia walked around her, tapping a finger to her chin. "If you have the time, I'd prefer to shorten the sleeves a little. Also, it is wool, so it may not be suitable for the warm summer weather. It will be perfect for the cooler months."

"I'll leave the coat with you, but would prefer taking the blouse and skirt home today."

"That suits me fine, Miss Rousseau. I'll total your purchases while you change. Do you have boots?" Cynthia asked.

"Not the kind I'd need on a ranch."

"I don't carry them here, but Deke Arrington has them at the saddlery."

"Do you want to go by there before supper, Vangie?" Suzette asked.

"I'll stop by to see Deke tomorrow. Right now, I'm ready to take the purchases home and have supper."

Suzette's mouth tipped into a grin. "I was hoping you'd say that."

"I believe that's her." Reggie whispered the words to Merle from their position down the street from the millinery. "We've finally tracked her down. Too bad she's with another woman or I'd introduce myself."

"Don't be an idiot, Reggie. We must speak with her in private. Inside her home would be the most acceptable."

"*We* are not going to talk to Miss Rousseau, Merle."

"What do you mean?"

They stepped farther into the shadows, watching the women walk to the end of the street. "Come on. We need to see where they're going."

Following Reggie, Merle grabbed his arm. "What you do you mean we are not going to speak with her?"

Shrugging out of his brother's grasp, not answering, he continued on, staying far enough behind the women so they wouldn't notice. "I do believe we're close to locating where Miss Rousseau is living."

Frustrated with Reggie's behavior, Merle blew out a string of curses as he followed him to the end of the street. Stopping at the corner, they peered around, seeing the women enter a house at the end of the next street.

Glancing over his shoulder, Reggie offered a grim smile. "We've found where she lives without approaching Eustice."

Merle understood his meaning. The less people who knew of their interest, the better it was for them. Gripping Reggie's shoulder, he turned his brother to face him.

"I want to know what you mean about the both of us are not going to speak with her. You know I won't allow you to approach her alone."

Retrieving the photograph he'd taken from the dresser in their room, Merle let out a slow breath.

Staring at it, he found himself hoping Vangie would listen to reason and deliver the funds her father took. His brother didn't have much patience. None when it came to money. He'd witnessed Reggie strangle a man until unconscious, stab another in the thigh, cut off the finger of another. All because they refused to pay what they owed.

They'd all professed their innocence, swearing Reggie was mistaken in his calculations and they owed the Riordan brothers nothing. Their pleadings fell on deaf ears. No matter their reasons, Reggie found it necessary to dole out physical punishment. In Merle's mind, the penalty on each didn't equate to the crime they were accused of committing.

His stomach roiled at what punishment Reggie would exact on Vangie if she refused to hand over the money. Staring at the image, it wasn't the first time Merle wondered who spoke the truth in each instance. Did the men who professed innocence owe the money, or did his brother thrive on pain, inventing wrongs when there were none?

Although Reggie promised not to hurt her, Merle knew his brother's assurances were more often lies than truth. What sickened him more was how he'd stood by each time, failing to lift a hand to stop his brother's actions. He'd allowed him to exact punishment on men who were most likely blameless. Worse, Merle had begun to suspect Reggie enjoyed the sight of blood, the knowledge he could make men suffer.

As far as he knew, his brother had never hurt a woman. The thought gave him little comfort. Reggie had a quick temper, and when matched with his lack of patience, it would take little for him to treat a woman the same as those other poor souls.

"Merle? If you're finished with the photograph, I'd like it back."

Shaking his head to move from thoughts of Reggie's true nature, Merle handed it to him. "Recall your promise not to hurt Miss Rousseau?"

"Of course I do." Slipping the image into a pocket, Reggie leaned down, picking up his satchel.

"I won't let you break your word on this."

"I've no intention of that. She does owe us the money, though, and I plan to use whatever persuasion required to regain the funds."

Taking a step closer, Merle lowered his voice, his gaze burning into his brother's. "Any *persuasion* will not include hurting Miss Rousseau in any way. I've stood by before, letting you do whatever you felt necessary to obtain what was owed us. This woman is an innocent. Her father's sins are not her fault. Assuming he actually did swindle us."

Reggie's eyes widened, then narrowed, his grip tightening on the handles of the satchel. Merle had never questioned his actions or how he kept their ventures solvent. He'd certainly never doubted his honesty.

Without responding, he sidestepped Merle. Entering the Gold Dust Hotel, he took a few minutes to register, taking a single room for both of them. Taking the key, he headed upstairs, knowing Merle would be a few paces behind.

Shoving the door open, Reggie glanced around before placing his satchel on the bed. Removing his hat, he slipped off his jacket, placing both on hooks.

A noise behind him, then the closing of the door indicated Merle had followed him inside. Waiting until he set his bag down, Reggie turned on him.

In a few short steps, he had his brother against the wall, an arm across Merle's throat. "Are you accusing me of lying? Is that what you were implying outside?"

Struggling to get free, Merle's eyes bulged at the pressure against his windpipe. Refusing to succumb to his brother's abuse, he lifted his knee in one swift move, catching him in the groin.

A loud bellow burst from Reggie before he released his grasp to shield himself from further injury. Cursing, he whirled around, his back to Merle.

"Don't ever threaten me again, Reggie," he choked out, pressing fingers to his throat. "I've stood by while you've done some unspeakable things, but *no* more. Let this serve as a warning. If you hurt Miss Rousseau, you'll no longer be allowed to call me your brother."

Face still flushed from the assault, Merle adjusted his collar. "We now know where she lives. Apparently, she doesn't live alone, which creates more problems." Walking to the window, he stared at the house across the street.

By the time Reggie regained his breath and straightened, Merle had turned toward him. "We should stay to see if they leave again." The grating in his voice spoke of the pain he still felt. "We can watch her comings and goings from here. She'll never see us."

Stepping next to him, Reggie peered out. About to turn away, he stopped, his features stiff. "Look."

Leaning over his shoulder, Merle watched two men walk up the steps, one of them knocking. A moment later, the door flew open. Vangie stood inside, a broad smile crossing her face.

They couldn't hear what was said, but she pulled the door wide, ushering the two inside.

"Well. We may have more of a problem than we planned," Reggie said, dropping the curtain to look at Merle. "It seems getting the money from Miss Rousseau may be harder than we'd hoped."

Chapter Nineteen

"What a wonderful surprise, Cam. I'm so pleased you and Bram rode into town." Sitting in the parlor of Suzette and Bay's home, Vangie smiled at both men, holding her gaze on Cam a few moments longer than necessary. The tug she felt for the handsome rancher never lessened. Instead, his attraction increased each time she saw him.

"I'm hoping you've no plans for supper, lass."

Feeling her face heat, she fiddled with the sleeve of her dress. If her mother were still alive, she'd find it an inappropriate action for a woman of any station.

"I have no plans."

"Bram and I would be honored to escort you to supper." Cam looked at Suzette. "If you and Bay don't have plans, you're welcome to join us."

"Thank you, Cam, but Bay and I have plans this evening." Supper alone with her husband had become rare. With Vangie out, she planned to make the most of their time together.

Fingering the brim of his hat, Cam stood, holding a hand out to Vangie. "Are you ready, lass?"

Taking it, she flushed at the feel of his calloused, warm skin against hers. They'd often walked with her arm through his, and it had been wonderful. This was different. An odd rush of excitement moved through her, making her body hum with anticipation. Of what, she didn't know, which created another wave of confusing anticipation.

Vangie had meant to speak with Suzette about the strange feelings she had when around Cam, why the mere sight of him created an intense reaction. Did it mean something? Was it normal?

She and her mother had never discussed such things. Maybe they should've, although Vangie had a hard time imagining her mother had such reactions to her father. Their relationship had always been respectful but not affectionate, at least not in public. She'd never seen them hold hands the way Cam held hers now.

Reluctant to let go, knowing she needed her reticule and wrap, she squeezed his hand before slipping hers from his grasp. "Please excuse me for a moment."

Cam's gaze followed her departure, mesmerized by the sway of her hips, the way a few stray strands of hair brushed her face. Bram's slight cough tore his attention away from the woman he intended to be his wife and back to his cousin's face. If they'd been at the ranch, he'd have smacked the smirk right off it.

"I'm ready."

Shifting, a smile tipped the corners of his mouth. She'd done nothing except don a bonnet and retrieve her reticule, yet his breath caught. Vangie didn't need anything to make her more beautiful.

She slipped her arm through his, gracing him with a warm, expectant grin. Saying their goodbyes to Suzette, the three stepped into the early evening air, walking the short distance to the Feather River Restaurant.

Zeke greeted them at the door, ushering them to a table by the window. "Will anyone else be joining you tonight?"

"Not tonight," Cam said, waiting while Zeke pulled out Vangie's chair.

Once they were seated, Zeke handed them menus, asked about wine, and excused himself. Bram set down the menu after a cursory glance. "I'll be having the steak."

"You have steak almost every night at home, lad." Cam sat back when Zeke arrived with their wine.

Bram slanted a brow to match his cocky grin. "Aye, but this one comes with a sauce Ma doesn't make."

"Have you made your decisions?" Zeke asked while pouring wine for the three.

Cam and Bram looked at Vangie, but she didn't notice. Her attention had moved across the room to two men being seated. Dressed in clothes more suitable for businessmen than ranchers, she noticed similarities between the two. Hair color, fair skin, the slight tilt of their noses. Brothers? The thought had a ball of fear forming in her throat, her breath catching.

"Are you ready to order, lass?" Cam's question broke through the unwelcome thought the men might be the same men Eustice mentioned. The Riordan brothers.

Ignoring their odd looks, she made a selection, unable to keep her gaze from wandering back to the men.

After placing their orders, Cam leaned closer. "Are you all right, lass?"

Hearing the concern in his voice, she shifted her focus to him. "Do either of you know the men at the table across the room?"

"The ones who look similar?" Bram asked.

Her eyes widened. "You notice the resemblance, too?"

"Aye. I've never seen them before."

Cam continued watching them, not looking away when one of the men spotted him. "Do you think they're the men Eustice spoke about?"

"Could be. They're similar to the men he described."

When Cam began to rise, Vangie placed a hand on his arm to stop him. "What are you thinking of doing?"

"A friendly conversation with the lads. Nothing for you to worry about."

"I don't think that's a good idea, Cam. What if they take offense and start a ruckus?"

"I'll not be accusing them of anything, lass." Moving out of her grasp, Cam rose, walking across the room toward their table.

Before he reached it, an explosion rocked the front windows, followed by screams and cursing from the diners.

"Get down!" Zeke shouted, encouraging the people to drop under the tables.

By the time Cam turned around, Bram had pulled Vangie from her chair, shielding her body as they moved toward the back of the restaurant. Skirting tables and diners crouched on the floor, he joined them.

"You get her out the back door and to Bay's house." Bram gave Vangie a gentle push into Cam's arms before drawing his six-shooter from its holster. "I'm going to see what happened."

"Find Brodie or Sam."

Giving a quick nod at Cam's words, he followed them out the back door. Waiting until they crossed the street to Bay's house, Bram ran along the side of the building, his gun held in front of him. He glanced around when he reached the corner. The sheriff's office was on the main street, fifty feet from where he stood, watching as people slowly emerged from the various buildings.

Waving them back inside, Bram crossed the street. The sound of gunfire had him crouching, his body flinching at the low voice behind him.

"What happened?" Bay crouched behind him, a six-shooter in each hand. He'd been a gunslinger, hired gun for ranchers and anyone who would pay, before moving to Conviction at the urging of August Fielder.

"I don't know."

Griff moved behind Bay. When another round of gunfire sounded, the three moved toward the jail.

"It's the Bank of Conviction." Bram slipped around the corner, his back against the building as he moved past the storefronts.

Smoke streamed through the open front door of the bank. Two of Brodie's deputies, Seth and Alex, stood on the boardwalk, keeping those brave enough to gather several feet away from the bank.

Bram, Bay, and Griff ran across the street, holstering their guns as they reached the two deputies.

"Where are Brodie and Sam?" Bram asked while trying to look inside the bank.

Seth pointed around the corner. "They're out back. From what we've heard, two men entered the bank, locked the doors, and set off dynamite."

Alex motioned to a group determined to gape at the damage. "Destroyed the safe and most of the back of the bank. It's a wonder they got away with anything at all."

Brodie joined them, scowling at Harold Ivers, the owner of the weekly Conviction Guardian. He held up his hand in warning when he attempted to approach, the man grousing when Alex moved to block him. "Ollie Hansen was ready to ride out after them."

Bram chuckled, thinking of the bank manager who'd been in Conviction a short period of time. August had hired the slender, self-effacing man with a gentle voice that belied a strong character.

"Did they get a good look at the robbers?" Seth asked.

Brodie's mouth twisted into a grimace. "They wore bandanas. But the one Ollie said was the leader wore a hat and coat similar to what the gunman had on when he shot him in the street."

Bram's hands fisted at his sides. "The gypsy." It was an accusation, a promise of action.

"You'll not be going after them until we're certain." Brodie's hard voice allowed no argument. "We need Thane to remember what he saw before being shot."

The crowd behind them parted when Cam pushed past them to join the others. "Is anyone hurt?"

"Nae. By the time Sam and I got here, the two robbers had ridden off with some of the money. Most of it blew up with the vault or scattered around the bank." Brodie's voice rose with urgency. "Seth and Alex, we need to mount up and follow Sam."

"I'll be going with you, lad," Cam said, withdrawing his gun to check the cylinder.

Bram nodded. "Aye. I'll be going, too."

Cam looked at Bay. "Vangie is with Suzette at your house. I'll ask you to be protecting her."

Before Bay could respond, a shout had them turning to see Eustice running across the street.

"They're here." He bent over, panting.

"Who's here, lad?" Cam's stomach clenched, afraid he already knew the answer.

"The Riordan brothers. I saw them." Eustice straightened, his head bobbing up and down as he pointed in the direction he'd come.

"Where?" Cam asked.

"They were running toward Vangie's house."

"You're certain, lad?" Bram asked.

"Yes. I remember them. They're bad men."

Brodie stepped next to Cam. "You need to stay here with Bay and Griff, lad. Make sure Vangie is protected." Without waiting for a response, he motioned for his deputies and Bram. "Let's go."

Chapter Twenty

Bay shoved open the front door, rushing inside, gun positioned in front of him. Laughter from the kitchen had him, Griff, and Cam holstering their weapons. They'd seen no sign of the men Eustice saw on the street.

Hurrying in behind them, Eustice stopped, his shoulders relaxing at the sound of women's voices. "They aren't here."

"I'm going to look around outside." Griff returned to the front door, sliding the gun from its holster.

"I'll check upstairs, Cam. You and Eustice make sure the women are all right." Bay knew from experience how normal voices didn't always suggest the obvious. He disappeared up the stairs while Cam and Eustice headed to the kitchen.

Hearing their footsteps, Vangie and Suzette turned toward the door. Removing his hat, Cam let out a breath when he saw they were all right. Vangie closed the distance between them, setting a hand on his arm.

"What happened?"

Her bright blue eyes searched his, as if she were looking for more than an answer to the question. Every time he saw her, Cam realized how much he wanted her in his life. Wanted her as his wife. He just needed the right time and place to voice his intentions. Shaking away the thought, vowing to return to it soon, he settled his hand over hers.

"A couple lads robbed the bank. Sam followed them out of town. Brodie, Bram, and the deputies are following."

"Did Bay ride with them?" Concern etched Suzette's face, her hands clasped in front of her.

"Nae." Cam didn't want to frighten them with the possibility the Riordan brothers were in town. "Bay and Griff will be here soon."

The back door opening drew their attention, Cam's hand going to the handle of his gun. The tension eased when Griff stepped inside. He holstered his gun, removing his hat.

"Good evening, ladies."

Suzette cocked her head before giving him a quick hug. "What are you doing coming in the back, Griff?"

Glancing at Cam, seeing the slight shake of his head, he grinned. "It was easier than walking around to the front."

"Did you see them?" Eustice asked, unaware of the desire to keep the knowledge of the brothers quiet.

Suzette lifted a brow. "See who?"

"Apologies for being late." Bay entered the kitchen, moving past Eustice and Cam to put an arm around his wife's shoulders. "Did Cam tell you about the excitement at the bank?"

"Yes." She shifted toward Eustice. "Who were you talking about?"

The large man seemed to shrink into himself. Shoving his hands into his pockets, he stared at the floor.

"Eustice thought he might have seen two men similar to the Riordan brothers," Bay answered. "We searched the area, but didn't find them."

"Maybe I was wrong," Eustice said, still staring at his feet.

"But maybe you were right." Vangie's worried look landed on Eustice, then moved to Cam. "We know they're looking for me."

Cam settled an arm over her shoulders. "Nae, lass. We believe they may be looking for you. Perhaps they've given up by now."

"Do you believe that, Cam?"

As much as he didn't want to scare Vangie, he refused to lie to her. "Nae, lass. I think they will continue until they find you."

"Maybe they already have." She swallowed the growing lump of fear.

"It would be best if you stayed inside until we confirm whether the men Eustice saw are the Riordans," Bay said, expecting an argument.

"I can't stay cloistered away in the house all day, every day."

"You'll not have to." Features solemn, Cam turned her to face him. "You'll be staying at the ranch, lass."

Vangie rode next to Cam on her bay mare, Duchess, in a state of disbelief. Suzette, Bay, Griff, and Eustice had rallied at Cam's suggestion of her moving to the ranch. Well, not a suggestion, but a firm request.

Their pressure came from concern, a way to keep her out of the way and safe while they searched for the two men Eustice had seen. The fact they matched the description of the men in the restaurant confirmed the nagging feeling in her stomach. The Riordans were in Conviction and looking for her.

Bram, Brodie, and the deputies hadn't returned by the time she'd packed a satchel plus the saddlebags Bay had provided. Cam had insisted all she needed was a dress or two, but she hadn't wanted to appear unprepared for her stay at the ranch.

Suzette had helped her roll up three cotton dresses, an extra chemise, nightdress, stockings, two shawls, slippers, gloves, and a few other items, placing them inside the satchel. They filled the saddlebags with personal items. A brush, soap, rose water, lotion she'd brought from Grand Rapids, books, hair ribbons, a few pieces of jewelry, and a pouch with money she kept for emergencies. Not that she'd need the funds at Circle M.

"Where will I be staying?"

"There's an extra bedroom in my house, lass."

"It wouldn't be proper for me to stay with you, Cam." She jolted at his bark of laughter.

"Ma, Colin, Sarah, and Jamie will be there. You'll be well chaperoned, lass. If you're not comfortable there, we can have you stay with Quinn or Fletch."

Worrying her bottom lip, she reined Duchess closer to Cam. "I don't want to be a nuisance."

Stopping, he reached over and grabbed her reins. "You'll never be a nuisance, lass. I want you at the ranch, and not just to protect you from the Riordans."

Her heart squeezed as his meaning became clear. "No?"

Using his free hand, he leaned over, cupping the back of her neck to draw her close. Her eyes widened in surprise, but she didn't pull away when he brushed his lips over hers. A stuttering breath escaped her when he did it a second time and drew back, pleased at the look of pleasure on her face.

"Nae, lass." He stroked the back of his hand down her cheek before returning her reins. This wasn't the time to explain his intentions. After those kisses, he didn't believe she'd have any doubts about what he wanted.

Focusing on the trail ahead, he knew they'd be in complete darkness by the time they reached Circle M. "Stay next to me, Vangie. We aren't far from the ranch, but the trail narrows a little and it will be harder to see ahead."

Still feeling a little dazed from the kisses, she licked her lips. "All...right."

Hiding a grin at the unsteady tone of her voice, he reached over, taking her hand in his. He wished she'd taken his offer to leave her horse in town and ride with him. Touching her seemed more important than anything else right now. All because of the touch of his lips on hers, something he planned to do again soon.

Continuing along, he squeezed her hand, reluctantly letting it go when the trail became too narrow for two horses. "Stay right on Duke's tail, lass."

He glanced over his shoulder when she fell back, a sense of unease creeping through him. They weren't far from the gypsy camp. At night, it was easy to spot their fires, pinpoint their exact location. The odd time before the sun set was more difficult, but he continued to scan the area.

Journeying through two sweeping bends in the trail, he began to relax. Circle M was less than half a mile away. As the trail widened, he shifted in the saddle to look at her when the sharp crack of a rifle had him jumping to the ground. Rushing to Duchess, he grabbed Vangie around the waist, roughly dragging her down beside him.

Drawing his gun, he took hold of her hand, rushing into the concealment of bushes when a shot hit the ground next to them. Shoving her ahead, he spun around, firing twice in the direction he believed the shooter hid. The sharp sounds spooked the horses, which was fine with Cam. He didn't want the animals between them and the shooter.

Firing once more, he lunged toward Vangie, covering her body with his. "Don't move, lass, and stay quiet."

The look she shot him indicated she planned to do neither. Another rifle shot tore into a slender pine, sending pieces of bark flying. When she lifted her head to look, he ruthlessly pushed her back down an instant before another bullet pierced the trunk.

Cam fired twice more, then grabbed Vangie's hand. "We have to get into the cover of the trees. Get in front of me."

Scrambling to her feet, she did as he asked, stumbling on a hidden root. Feeling a firm hand steady her, she moved as fast as possible given the heavy boots and billowing shirt. When she began to tire, Cam stepped beside her, wrapping an arm around her waist to keep her moving.

Guiding them between jagged bushes, he made a quick turn, then another, putting distance and darkness between them and the person who wanted them dead. Crouching down, he positioned Vangie behind him before reloading his gun.

A minute passed, then several more without any indication they'd been followed. Cam didn't relax. He waited until they were cloaked in complete darkness before leaning down to whisper into her ear.

"I need to find out if he left."

She gripped his arm, fingers digging into the fabric of his shirt. "No, Cam. We're safe here."

"We don't know that, lass. He may be moving around behind us."

"All the more reason for you to stay here. If you move, he'll know where we're hiding."

"I need to find the horses so we can get to the ranch."

Sucking in a deep breath, then blowing it out, she nodded. "Then I'm coming with you."

"Nae, lass. You'll be safer here."

"If you go, I go." Her voice was filled with unbending determination.

"It's too dangerous."

"I'll be safe with you, Cam. Safer than hiding out here alone." This time he heard the quiver of fear in her voice.

"It won't be easy without moonlight."

He was close enough to see a slight grin curve the corners of her mouth. "There's a sliver. Besides, I don't intend to die out here. I'm too excited about staying at the ranch to let anything spoil it."

Stifling a harsh chuckle, he shook his head in amusement, accepting she'd follow if he left her behind. "All right, lass, but you'll be sticking right with me. If I give an order, you obey it without question."

She waited a moment before nodding.

"I'll be having your word on that, Vangie."

Shoving to her feet, she bent at the waist to keep herself at the same height as the bushes. "Fine. You're in charge."

Unable to resist, he leaned close, covering her mouth with his. Given their circumstances, it was stupid and perfect. The best kiss he'd ever had, and it was with the woman he intended to make his. Pulling back, he rested his forehead against hers.

"You'll take hold of my belt and not let go. Do you understand, lass?"

Gripping his belt, she tightened her hold, steeling her resolve. "Let's get out of here."

Chapter Twenty-One

Circle M

Fletcher MacLaren ran toward the barn, changing directions when he spotted Quinn and Colin riding in from a day with the herd.

"Gunshots," he shouted, pointing in the direction of the trail from town. As he did, the sharp, but distant crack of a rifle echoed. "Hear it?"

"Aye." Colin reined Chieftain in a circle, then rode toward the southernmost corral. Quinn came up beside him, both waiting for Fletcher to saddle Domino and join them.

"It will be dark soon." Quinn scanned the area, holding his stallion, Warrior, steady. "The gypsies?"

"Could be. Bram and Cam are in town." Colin knew Quinn would understand his concern. "They'd be coming home about now."

"Aye." Quinn's jaw clenched at what might be happening so close to the ranch.

"Let's go, lads." Fletcher streaked past them, slowing up at Colin's shout.

"We need to be careful, lad. It could be hunters."

"You're not believing that, are you, Colin?" Fletcher asked.

"Nae. But we'll not be riding into something until we know the danger, Fletch." Colin glanced at Quinn, who nodded. Another shot cracked through the darkening forest. "Come on."

Colin took the lead. As the oldest, even if only by months, he felt a responsibility for those younger. They rode in the direction of the shots, guns drawn, shoulders tense.

One more rifle shot was followed by the pops of a six-shooter.

"Not hunters." Colin kicked Chieftain, concern building. His gut told him Cam and Bram were in danger, being stalked. Perhaps by the man who'd shot Thane.

A few more shots had them increasing their pace, veering to the right.

"Hold up." Colin held his hand in the air. Just off the trail ahead were two horses.

"It's Duke and Duchess." Fletcher closed the distance between him and the animals, talking in a low voice as he got closer.

Neither horse shied away at his approach. Nor when he grabbed their reins. His throat tightened, heart pounding at what it could mean. Cam wouldn't let his horse go unless he'd been attacked. The presence of Duchess had to mean Vangie was with him.

Flipping the horses' reins over a low branch, he slid to the ground, removing his rifle from the scabbard. Behind him, his cousins did the same.

"Spread out, lads," Colin said. "Duke would never stray far from Cam."

Guns ready, they searched the area, moving north in a wide arc. They didn't call out, not wanting to draw attention from the shooter who'd targeted Cam and Vangie.

The sky continued to darken as they walked west, toward town. The only sounds were those made by their boots on the hard ground and the wind rustling through branches laden with leaves.

The absence of further gunfire didn't lull them into lowering their guard. Someone had fired at a member of their family. They had no idea if there was one shooter or more.

Too many questions and no answers. All they cared about was finding Cam and Vangie.

They'd searched for close to half an hour before Colin heard the sound of someone moving through the brush. Cupping his hands to his mouth, he blew an intricate whistle, calling Fletcher and Quinn to return. As young boys, they'd perfected the call, using it when in danger.

Fletcher and Quinn whistled back. Then a third call wafted through the trees.

Cam.

Rushing toward the last call, Colin huffed out a relieved breath. Cam held Vangie around the waist, but they were alive.

Rushing toward them, he wrapped his arms around both. "Are you all right?"

"Other than wanting to find the person shooting at us, aye."

"What happened?" Colin asked, already suspecting there were no answers other than the fact someone tried to kill them.

Cam grinned when he saw Quinn and Fletcher, then explained the attack to all three. "Then the shots stopped. I don't know if it was one lad or more."

"Did you see anyone?" Vangie hadn't spoken until now, too shaken from the attack.

"Nae, lass. We may have spooked whoever shot at you." Colin nodded behind him. "The horses are close. We should get you home and let the uncles know what happened."

"My guess is the same man who shot Thane tried to kill you," Quinn said, the familiar ache of seeing his brother struggle to recover piercing his chest.

"Aye, but we've no proof." Cam threaded his fingers through Vangie's. "We need to get the lass away from here. Then we need to go hunting ourselves."

Brodie stalked into the jail early the next morning, still fuming at the way the robbers had eluded them. Sam had done his best to keep them in sight, but lost them when the two split up. The posse had caught up with him miles south of town. The sun had set, making it too dark to continue the search.

Lowering himself into his chair, he reached into a drawer, pulling out a stack of wanted posters. He wanted to show them to the bank manager and his employees. Maybe one of them would recognize something. A scar, mustache, thick brows.

He looked up when the door opened, expecting to see one of his deputies. Instead, his younger brother walked in.

"Fletch." Brodie stood, pulling him into a hug. "What brings you to town, lad?" That was when he saw the lines of worry etched in his face.

"Cam and Vangie were shot at on their way to the ranch last night. They weren't far from the gypsy camp."

The words had Brodie grabbing his hat and moving to the door. "Are they hurt?"

"Nae. Colin, Quinn, and I heard the shots and rode out. They were less than a mile from the ranch."

Opening the door, Brodie headed outside, Fletcher behind him. "One shooter?"

"We don't know. Ma and the aunts are real worried. We thought you might want to take a look around and talk to the gypsies."

"I'll be taking Sam, Seth, and Alex with me. I need to let Jack now we'll be gone." The first deputy hired, Jack Perkins, preferred to stay in town, which suited the others fine. "It may not be the gypsies, Fletch."

"Aye, you're probably right. Cam's thinking it might be the Riordan brothers."

Brodie's brow rose at the name. "Eustice thought he'd seen them. That's why I didn't want Cam going after the robbers with us."

"According to Cam and Vangie, Eustice *insists* he saw them. Plus, the lass believes she spotted them in the Feather River Restaurant when she, Cam, and Bram were having supper."

They walked together along the boardwalk, watching for Sam, Seth, and Alex. "Killing Vangie won't get them the money they think she has."

"Aye, but killing Cam might."

Brodie stopped, placing fisted hands on his hips. "They're wanted for fraud and embezzlement, not murder. I'd be having a hard time believing they'd kill for the money."

"Aye, but we don't know how much money the lads want," Fletcher said. "If they were watching Bay's house, they would've seen Cam and Vangie leave. It would've been easy to follow them."

Brodie considered his brother's words, understanding the logic. Except for his belief murder seemed extreme. As Fletcher said, the amount would matter to men such as the Riordans. Men who would travel across country to stalk their target.

"Is everyone at the ranch?" He continued along the boardwalk, waving when he saw Seth and Alex step out of the Gold Dust.

"Aye. Vangie is staying in Aunt Kyla's house." Fletcher shook his head, thinking of the irony. "The reason Cam took her out of town was to get her away from the Riordans." He shook their outstretched hands when the deputies joined them.

Brodie explained the situation. He knew the two deputies were as frustrated as him at losing the bank robbers. They'd welcome the order to ride toward Circle M to check the area where they believed the shooter had hidden.

"Do you want me to find Sam?" Fletcher asked.

"He'll be at home with Jinny. I told him to take the day off."

"Sam will want to be a part of this, Brodie."

"Aye, the lad will. We'll meet you both at the jail and ride out." When Fletcher turned to find Sam, Brodie called after him. "Find Bay and Griff. They'll be wanting to know about what happened."

195

"Where the hell were you, Reggie?" Merle had been pacing the room since early morning, angry and frustrated to find his brother missing.

They'd watched until the men entered the house after the robbery. If the four men hadn't come along, Vangie would already be in their care, answering questions about her father and the missing money.

"I spent the night at the Gold Dust."

"You took another room when we're already paying for this one?"

"Hell no," Reggie ground out. He was tired and still shaken from the activities of the night before. He hoped Merle didn't notice. "I drank a little, played cards, and went upstairs with one of the women."

Merle could see the lie in his brother's eyes. Reggie might occasionally seek the company of a saloon woman, but he *never* stayed the night.

"What aren't you telling me?"

"There's nothing else." He had no intention of telling Merle he'd left the saloon early, returning to the house where Vangie lived.

Not long after arriving, she'd emerged with one of the men. Eustice had come out right afterward, taking hurried steps to the livery. Reggie followed the three, realizing what must be happening.

Cursing at not having a horse or rifle, he'd done what he believed any other man would have. He stole both and followed. The rest still had him shaking inside.

Merle paced to the window, looking out on the house below. "She'll have to come out sometime."

Reggie didn't correct him. His brother had no idea she'd already ridden out the night before with one of the men. Instead, he decided to deflect further questions.

"We should get breakfast and decide what to do next."

Merle glared at him a long moment before grabbing his hat off a hook. "There's not much to decide. The woman is never alone. We either have to go through Eustice to get to her or take her from the house." He sent Reggie a meaningful look. "Or we could put this all behind us and go home."

"We've spent weeks of time and a good deal of money to get here. I'm not giving up on getting back what we're owed."

"Eustice would rather die than help us get to her."

Reggie knew Merle was right. That wasn't the way he planned to handle it, though.

"We'll take him, then get word to her that if she doesn't agree to meet us, she'll never see him again."

"I don't like it, Reggie. We agreed not to harm anyone."

"No, Merle. We agreed not to harm Evangeline. We said nothing about Eustice."

Chapter Twenty-Two

Belcher Grey hadn't slept the night before. Everything he'd worked to achieve was at risk and he needed to find a way to put it right. He'd lost control of his family, one member in particular.

Jean-Paul Baptista Heron had been born into the family, grown up with the same love as everyone else. Along the way, the happy, gregarious young boy had lost his parents and sister in an accident. The happiness fled, the gregarious nature replaced with a wary suspicion.

Still, he'd become a valuable member of the group. Jean-Paul trained himself to be an expert hunter, providing food when others came back to the camp empty-handed. Slender, with dark hair and prominent nose, he was no more than five-ten. His ruddy complexion spoke to days in the sun and long nights consuming as much whiskey as possible before passing out. At least the nights he stayed in camp. Last night, he hadn't.

Belcher knew something had broken inside the man. Jean-Paul had become consumed in darkness, become a loner, shunning the celebrations common in the family. He'd ignored his odd actions the last couple years, as they hadn't put the family in danger. Things had changed since erecting their camp close to the MacLaren property.

The sound of horses approaching had him moving toward the north edge of the camp, the closest point of the trail leading from town to the Circle M. Ever since the gunfire last night, he'd been expecting either the MacLaren men or the sheriff to arrive. Perhaps both, since the sheriff was a MacLaren.

Back straight, bland expression on his face, he waited. A few men from camp joined him, but most were out hunting. He counted seven men, Brodie MacLaren being the only one he recognized. As they got closer, he identified four wearing badges. He didn't budge when they reined their horses less than a couple feet away.

Brodie glanced at Belcher before his gaze moved to the men beside him and the rest of the camp. "Mr. Grey."

"Sheriff."

"I'll be needing to ask you some questions."

Belcher held his hands in front of him, palms up. "Ask."

"Did you hear gunshots last night? It would've been close to sundown."

"Yes."

"Do you know who fired them?"

"No."

"They were aimed at a man and woman riding from town to Circle M."

Belcher's jaw tensed, his only reaction. "Were they hurt?"

"Nae. But from what we know, the shooter was trying to kill them."

The corner of one eye twitched before Belcher glanced away, then turned toward his men. "Do any of you know something about the gunshots?"

Some crossed their arms, others took a step away. All shook their heads.

"We cannot help you, Sheriff."

Brodie wasn't surprised. He'd expected nothing from the gypsies, but wasn't ready to ride away. His gut told him someone from this camp had been the one to fire on Cam and Vangie. Signaling to his deputies to follow his lead, Brodie dismounted.

"We'll be looking around."

Belcher's shoulders tensed, but he stepped aside. "You'll find nothing."

Brodie motioned for his men to spread out. They already knew what to look for, which included speaking with anyone who would talk to them.

Fletcher, Bay, and Griff stayed on their horses, their focus alternating between the camp and the men in front of them. None were armed, which meant nothing. The wagons used as homes could hold several men each, and all of them could be brandishing weapons.

Minutes passed as Brodie and his deputies made a thorough search. Belcher didn't make any move to follow them. He wouldn't argue about entering the wagons. They had nothing to hide.

As Brodie and his men searched, Bay reined his horse to skirt the outside of the camp, unable to sit and watch any longer. He wanted to make certain no one ran off while confirming no wagons or horses were positioned for a quick escape. The route would also give him a chance to look for tracks from more than one rider.

Twenty minutes passed before Brodie returned, a leather pouch in one hand. He strode straight up to Belcher, his gaze never wavering from the older man.

"Do you want to tell me about this?" Brodie opened the bag, pulling out a wad of bills, most scorched and torn, as if they'd been through an explosion.

Belcher didn't reach for them. "I've never seen those before." He turned toward his men. "Have any of you seen this?"

As before, the men shook their heads, saying nothing.

"Show me where you found it."

Sliding the bills back into the pouch, Brodie retraced his steps to an older wagon. An elderly woman sat on a stool outside, paying no attention to the men, the same as when Sam had searched her wagon. He stood next to the door, arms crossed, saying nothing about the additional pouches he'd discovered. At Brodie's order, they now resided in the pockets of his coat.

"Does anyone live with her?" Brodie walked up the steps to enter the wagon, Belcher following.

"We all share what we have when needed."

Brodie moved farther into the darkened space, bending to lift a small, carved box. A slot existed to insert a key, but it was unlocked. He handed it to Belcher.

"This is where we found the money. There were several bags. One of my deputies is holding the others. Do you have any idea who would've left them in the woman's wagon if she lives alone?"

Belcher studied the empty box as if he'd never seen it before, turning it over. He shrugged, handing it back. "I have no answers for you."

"This wagon is owned by the elderly lass outside?"

Belcher's wary eyes shifted to the door, then back to Brodie. "Yes."

Blowing out a breath, he shook his head. "That's too bad. I'd hoped someone else might be responsible for hiding stolen money from the bank robbery. I'll be taking her back with us to the jail."

Belcher's eyes went wide, his jaw tightening. "You are arresting her?"

"I've no choice. We found stolen money in her wagon and you've told me no one shares the space with her." He moved past Belcher, toward the steps. "You may visit her."

He nodded at Sam when he landed on the ground. The woman made no protest when his deputy helped her up, loosely winding a short, smooth cord around her wrists. He'd found it inside her wagon. It was the kind used to tie back draperies.

"You cannot take her to jail."

Brodie ignored Belcher's protest. "Aye, I can. She owns the wagon where we found stolen bills. You can hire an attorney. I'll be guessing the trial will take place within a few days."

They followed Sam as he escorted the woman through the camp and toward their horses. Brodie assumed he'd put the woman in front of him for the journey to town. She was short and slender, weighing no more than a hundred pounds. For some reason, Brodie doubted she was as frail as she appeared.

Her eyes were alert, mouth twisted in a tight scowl. She made no attempt to escape. When he stopped next to his horse, Seth came forward, allowing Sam to mount. When settled, Seth lifted her to sit in front of him.

"Wait." Belcher moved forward, waving his arms. "You can't take her. She is old and sick."

"The lass appears fine to me." Brodie walked to his own horse and swung into the saddle. He stared down at Belcher, moving his gaze over the others who'd gathered close by. "We'll be taking good care of her, Mr. Grey."

They rode out, Bay bringing up the rear after making certain no one went for a weapon. There'd be no bullets in the back today.

Belcher raged through the camp, cursing, questioning, trying to discover how the money got into the widow's wagon. She was a tough woman, would handle being in jail fine, but if he didn't learn the truth, she could be sent to prison. Which would be where she'd die.

No one had answers. Whoever had stowed the money in the carved box had entered and left without anyone seeing them. It meant they came in late at night when the camp was quiet.

He always posted a guard, but more often than not, they'd doze off. Belcher questioned the man who'd been watching the camp the night before. It was as expected. The man had seen nothing.

While moving from wagon to wagon, the rest of the men had returned, surprised at what had transpired during their absence. Two were still missing. Jean-Paul and another man who often hunted with him.

Belcher's gut twisted, heart plummeting. Without questioning them, he knew they'd been the ones to rob the bank. They may have also been the ones to shoot at the man and woman from Circle M.

He didn't want to believe it, but there were no other answers. Not unless others from the outside had robbed the bank and tried to kill the couple. A voice in Belcher's head shouted that wasn't what happened.

All he could do now was wait for their return. Then there'd be hell to pay.

Circle M

Cam watched from the corral as Vangie swept the porch of one house, then another. She'd woken early, helped his mother prepare breakfast, and hadn't stopped since. He could only imagine the blisters she'd have by supper.

She looked up, resting against the handle of the broom. Spotting him, she waved, a broad smile on her face. It felt like a kick to his gut.

"The lass is going to fit in fine, Cam."

He turned at the sound of Colin's voice. "Aye, she will." Pride filled him at his older brother's comment. "I'm hoping she'll want to stay after the danger passes."

Throwing his head back, Colin laughed. "The lass will want to stay wherever you are. I'd suggest you be thinking about asking her to marry you."

Cam hesitated. He knew how he felt about Vangie, but didn't know her feelings for him.

"You *have* told her how you feel, right, lad?"

Tensing, Cam pursed his lips. "Nae, I haven't."

"Ach. You need to be doing that. And soon. We've already got one wedding to plan. It would be no hardship to plan another."

Colin referred to the upcoming wedding of their mother, Kyla, and August Fielder. August had come to him and Cam a few weeks before, stating his intentions. They'd sent a telegram to their middle brother, Blaine, who took care of their ranch near Settlers Valley. No one objected, although Cam struggled with their mother leaving the ranch.

Once she'd assured them of her and August's intention to return to the ranch on Fridays and stay over the weekend, his mind had eased. It didn't matter she'd be a short distance away in Conviction. Cam preferred her to be where she'd be under his protection.

When Brodie and Sam insisted they would watch over her, he'd calmed further, accepting the inevitable. Their mother would be marrying August and moving on with her life.

It seemed time he did the same.

"Aye. It's time I spoke with Vangie about my feelings, and hope the lass feels the same."

Slapping him on the back, Colin grinned. "Lad, I've never seen a woman more in love than Vangie. She's a bonny lass with a big heart. You two are going to be very happy."

Cam swallowed the lump building in his throat. Colin was right. He could finally see his future, and it definitely included the beautiful woman working twenty yards away.

Chapter Twenty-Three

"Did you find him?" Belcher stalked to the search party who'd been asked to find Jean-Paul. By the look on their faces, he could guess the answer.

Several shook their heads while one stepped forward, massaging the back of his neck. "We found no sign of him, or Turner."

Jean-Paul had returned a week before with a stranger. A short, stout man with a ragged scar across his face. Turner spoke little, and his surly manner didn't invite questions. When Belcher told Jean-Paul the outsider couldn't stay, Turner camped a hundred yards away. Now both men were missing.

"His camp?" Belcher asked.

"There's nothing there. I'm certain whatever Jean-Paul is doing includes Turner."

Belcher found himself agreeing. "We must be ready when they return."

"We will be."

Watching the group disperse, Belcher tried to ignore the sick feeling in his stomach. It had grown worse since the sheriff's visit and the discovery of the money pouches. He needed to ride into town and talk to the woman they'd arrested. Belcher knew she hadn't stolen the money, but was certain she knew who did.

She'd always had a special place in her heart for Jean-Paul, providing food and a place to keep his few belongings after his parents died. They'd grown close over the years. When he'd started hunting for the family of gypsies, the first person who received a portion was the widow. The rest went to Belcher, who divided it among everyone else.

Rolling a cigarette, he considered what needed to be done. They protected their own while doling out their own form of justice to those who put the family in danger. If Belcher's instincts were correct, Jean-Paul had not only stolen money, but tried to kill one of the MacLarens and the woman with him. Actions which put the entire camp in danger. It didn't matter Belcher's personal feelings. The family couldn't tolerate such activities.

It didn't mean they'd turn him or Turner over to the sheriff. If they were found guilty, the family would dole out their own form of justice.

Taking a last puff on the cigarette, Belcher tossed it to the ground, stomping the stub with the heel of his boot. Unable to put off the trip any longer, he strode to his horse, saddled it, and mounted.

"Are you going to the jail?" one of the family asked as they walked toward him.

"Yes. Maybe she'll talk to me."

"I'll go with you, Belcher."

He gave a quick shake of his head. "I'm going alone. Everyone else needs to stay in camp in case

Jean-Paul and Turner return. Say nothing, but make certain they don't leave."

The man shoved his hands into his pockets, letting out a slow breath. "You're not considering turning them in, are you?"

"Have we ever let outsiders settle our problems?" Belcher reined his horse toward town.

"No."

"We won't start now."

Circle M

Cam finished a training session with one of their colts, his gaze wandering to Vangie. She'd attached a rug to the clothesline, using a broom to beat out the dust.

"The lass hasn't stopped since she woke at sunrise." Quinn stood next to him, holding open the gate to the corral so Cam could pass by with the colt. "Maybe you should be thinking of giving her a break. Take her on a ride toward the river."

Cam knew what Quinn hinted at. The same as Colin, except his brother had been more open about it. Both thought the time had come for him to ask Vangie to marry him. He agreed, but hadn't found the courage to say the words. Cam hadn't even admitted he loved her.

"Let me take care of the colt while you talk with the lass." Quinn reached out, taking the lead rope. When Cam didn't move, Quinn shoved his shoulder. "Off with you, lad."

He looked down at his pants and shirt, something he rarely did when working. They were covered in dust, his boots showing the evidence of working with horses. Knowing brushing off his clothes would do nothing, he looked up to see Vangie taking down one rug and replacing it with another.

She wore an old cotton bonnet over her hair, a bandanna protecting her face from the dust. His mother had given her a pair of gloves, a complete change from the silk ones he'd seen her wear in town. When Vangie turned around, catching him staring, he felt the sharp punch to his gut when a smile brightened her face.

Tearing off his gloves, he tossed them toward the barn, then walked toward her. Stopping within a few feet, he shoved his hands into his pockets so as not to reach out for her. He wanted nothing more than to take her hand, lead her where no one could watch, and kiss her. Deeply, thoroughly, like he'd wanted to do since the day they'd met.

"You've been working most of the day, lass."

She looked between him and the rug, the broom still in her hand. "I don't know how your mother and the women do it. The work seems to go on and on."

He didn't miss the flash of a grin. "Is it too much for you?"

Dropping the broom, she crossed her arms, brow arching. "Not at all. After this, I plan to work a while in the garden before helping Kyla with supper."

"Nae, lass. You'll be going on a ride with me."

"But—"

"You'll not be arguing with me. You need a rest and I need to get away for a spell."

Hearing hoofs on the hard ground, he turned. Quinn walked toward them holding the reins of Duke and Duchess. They'd already been saddled.

Staring down at her soiled dress and dirty hands, Vangie touched her bonnet, wincing at how she must appear. "I should clean up and change clothes."

Reaching out, Cam grabbed her hand, tugging her down the steps toward the horses. "Thanks, Quinn." He helped Vangie into the saddle, then handed her the reins for Duchess.

"You'll be riding to the river?"

"Aye. Will you let the others know we'll be back in a couple hours?"

Nodding, Quinn waved before heading back to the barn. Swinging up on Duke, Cam reined him north. "Come on, lass."

He felt a rush of excitement at showing her one of his favorite spots along the river. Not once in the years they'd owned the ranch had Cam invited a woman to ride along with him. No other woman had ever been his guest at Circle M.

Quinn had been the man he emulated when it came to women. At least before his cousin had married Emma Pearce. Cam had been surprised at how easily he'd made the adjustment from being an enthusiastic bachelor to settling down with one woman.

After meeting Vangie, Cam understood the reason for Quinn's change. Other women no longer held any appeal. They hadn't to Quinn and they no longer did to Cam.

Reining to a stop at the top of a hill, he pointed north. "Everything you see is part of Circle M."

"Your mother talked about a ranch near Settlers Valley."

"Aye. My brother, Blaine, runs it."

"I don't recall meeting him."

"The lad doesn't come home often. He and his wife, Lia, are busy keeping the ranch going. My cousin, Heather, is married to Caleb Stewart. Their ranch is close to Blaine's. The Settlers Valley sheriff, Nate Hollis, used to be a deputy for Brodie. He's now married to Geneen, Sarah's sister."

Vangie worked to keep the names straight before her eyes widened. "Oh yes. Sarah did mention how much she misses her. She and Colin are hoping to ride north for a visit soon."

Cam leaned on the saddle horn, continuing to stare ahead. "Sarah and Colin have been talking about it for over a year. I've a feeling we'll all be getting together soon."

"Oh?"

"Aye. You've heard Ma and August Fielder will be marrying."

"Sarah, Kyla, and I have talked about the wedding. It's only a month off, yet your mother seems so calm about it. If it were me, I'm certain I'd be nervous."

Cam thought about his father, Angus. How he and his mother had been so much in love. He'd doubted she'd ever considered marrying again. August was a good man, and Cam was glad they'd found each other.

"Ma and Da were married a long time. They'd been in love since they were bairns in Scotland."

Vangie's features sobered. She knew what it was like to lose family. "I heard about how he and your uncle Gillis were murdered. It must've been awful for you."

"It was hard on all of us, but especially for Ma and Aunt Audrey."

"Has Audrey thought of marrying again?"

"I've no idea. Bram would be happy for her, though. I'm thinking Quinn and Thane would be, too. She'd have to spend more time in town to meet someone, and Aunt Audrey rarely rides in. She prefers staying at the ranch. Like Ma and Da, she and Uncle

Gillis fell in love when they were young. It took her months to get over his death."

"Maybe watching Kyla and August marry will encourage her to meet someone. She's still young and quite beautiful. So many men would be proud to settle down with her."

Straightening, he looked at her. "You think so, lass?"

"Being beautiful? Absolutely."

"Nae. I mean men would be interested in her."

She shot him an odd look, as if he'd lost his mind. "I think Doctor Vickery is quite interested in her. Did you see the way he looked at her after Thane was shot? He's definitely smitten with her. I think he's working on the courage to ask about courting her. Maybe he'll find it at the wedding. He will be invited, won't he?"

"I'm guessing most of the town will be invited, lass. August doesn't do anything small. Are you ready to ride on?"

Smiling, she nodded. "Whenever you are."

They rode in silence toward the river, Cam thinking about Doc Vickery trying to find the courage to approach Aunt Audrey. He faced the same dilemma with Vangie.

Cam had thought of little else the last few days. He should've talked to Quinn or Fletcher about how they'd approached Emma and Maddy. It was too late now.

By the time they left the river for the ranch, Vangie would have no doubt about his feelings.

Chapter Twenty-Four

The Riordans kept watch on Bay's house from their room in the hotel, Reggie becoming more agitated as each hour passed. There'd been no sign of Vangie since the night before. It was now late afternoon.

He'd said nothing to Merle about following Cam and Vangie out of town, or the theft of the horse and rifle. Reggie had returned both, but not to their original location.

Merle crossed his arms, leaning against the wall. "We can't wait around forever. She may have gone to San Francisco or Sacramento."

"It's been less than twenty-four hours. We wait." Reggie sat on the bed, staring down at his hands, thinking.

They needed to be careful. Time was closing in on them. It wouldn't be long before they'd be forced to forget the money and return east. He'd said nothing of this to Merle. His brother would push to leave now rather than spend a few more days coming up with a plan.

Reggie already knew the plan. It involved taking Eustice, holding him someplace away from town, and sending a message to Vangie. She'd have no choice but to give the Riordans whatever they wanted. He glanced up at movement across the room.

Shoving away from the wall, Merle stalked across the room to the door. "I'm going for a drink. You can stay here and keep watch."

Before Reggie could answer, his brother slammed the door on his way out of the hotel. Cursing under his breath, he took one more look out the window at Bay's house, then grabbed his hat. There were things he needed to do before joining Merle at the saloon.

Hurrying down the hotel stairs, Reggie rushed along the boardwalk, past the Feather River Hotel, Cynthia Abbott's millinery, a couple more shops, and another saloon.

Pushing his hat low on his forehead, he hustled through Chinatown, glancing up every now and then. Mainly, he kept to himself, not wanting to garner any attention lest someone remember him passing through the tightly packed area.

Reggie had been told Chinatown emerged a few years after Conviction began to grow. They came to work the nearby gold mines, venturing into commerce when the mines played out or they became too old to work the long hours to enhance the pockets of others.

Reaching the end of the boardwalk, he looked up, staring across the open expanse of road to the blacksmith and livery. From talking to locals, he knew there was an apartment above the structure. He'd heard it was scorching hot in the summer and somewhat more pleasant in the winter. It all depended on how much the forge was used, if it was fired up each day or infrequently. It took a special person to work and live in such conditions.

Crossing the street, he stopped to read a hand carved sign hanging on the blacksmith door.

Back in two hours.

Reggie groaned at the primitive message. No indication when Eustice had left, only the terse message he'd return in two hours. That could mean a difference between one minute and a hundred and twenty. He could stay close and wait, or locate Merle. Neither appealed to him.

Reggie found himself retracing his steps, then turning onto the main street. Before him stood the Western Union office. It also served as the town's post office. It had been too long since he'd sent word to his wife. Less time since sending a telegram to his mistress.

Today, he'd mail a short letter to both, informing each he'd soon be on his way home. Then he'd ride west, toward Circle M.

Circle M

Cam reined to a stop next to the river and slid to the ground. Helping Vangie out of her saddle, he took her hand, walking to the edge of the water.

They stood in silence for several minutes, watching the river make its way toward town and the main section of the Feather River. It was summer, warm days giving way to cooler nights, but not uncomfortably so.

Squeezing her hand, he let go. "I'll get a blanket."

Vangie watched him leave, feeling more at peace and content than she had in a long time. Staying at the ranch had been an excellent idea. She didn't mind the work. It gave her time to get to know Cam and his family.

Hearing boots crunch the dried leaves, she turned, seeing the smile on his face. Broad-shouldered, muscled, and handsome, she swallowed at the intensity of his gaze. She wasn't sure what it meant, but it was different than what she'd seen in the past.

Spreading the blanket on the ground, he again took her hand and helped her down. "This is one of my favorite places on the ranch."

Tucking her legs under her, she didn't let go of his hand. "It's beautiful. I can see why you like coming here."

"Most of the trees lose their leaves in the fall, but fill out in early spring. Then the wildflowers bloom. They don't last long, and I missed them this year, but next year, we'll ride out so I can show you."

Her heart leapt at the idea he believed she'd still be around in a year. Maybe this meant he wanted more. Perhaps as much as she did.

"You've been working hard, lass. I didn't bring you to the ranch for you to work."

"I don't mind at all. In fact, I'm tired of sitting around, doing needlework, shopping, and reading. I'd even thought of getting a job to pass the time."

Cam knew she didn't need the money and understood her need to do more than wait around for Suzette to complete her work at the restaurant. He'd wondered why she hadn't visited San Francisco. Until now, he hadn't considered she might not want to go alone. Cam knew he could fix that.

"I've been needing to go to San Francisco for business." He cleared his throat, a tinge of uneasiness threading through him. "Would you be wanting to go with me, lass?"

Her eyes flashed, the invitation coming as a surprise. "I would love to go, but it wouldn't be proper. Not unless I could talk Suzette into going with us."

Shifting to face her, he stroked a finger down her cheek. "You'll not be needing a chaperone, lass."

Heart pounding, Vangie searched his face, not understanding. "Of course I would, Cam. It wouldn't be right to travel with a man who isn't family."

"Aye. But it would be fine with your husband."

Breath catching, she felt her face heat. "Husband?"

"I've been in love with you for a long time, lass. Since the first moment we met, I knew you were the woman I wanted in my life." Taking both her hands between his, he met her expectant gaze. "Marry me, lass."

Lips parting, she continued to stare at him, moisture building in her eyes. "You want to marry me?"

The question was so tentative, filled with doubt, he almost grinned. "Is it such a surprise, lass?" Leaning forward, he brushed a kiss over her lips. "Tell me you've never thought of this."

A nervous chuckle burst through her lips, a smile forming on her face. "I've thought of it many times, Cam."

Hovering above her mouth, he closed the distance, kissing her again. This time was longer, more intimate, before he pulled away.

"Marry me," he whispered.

"All right."

An instant later, a gunshot had them jerking away. A bullet hit the ground a couple feet away, dirt and leaves bursting around them.

Shoving her to the ground, Cam covered her body with his. Reaching down, he pulled his gun from its holster, his head whipping around to scan the area as another shot hit the dirt less than two feet away.

"Cam?" Fear laced her voice.

"Stay down, lass. I'm trying to see where the shots are coming from." They were out in the open, in a small clearing next to the river. He leaned down next to her ear. "We need to move, lass."

Body trembling, she shook her head. "There's nowhere to go."

"Behind the trees where he'll not have a clear shot." When a third shot came even closer, he grabbed her hand, tugging her up, and ran.

He didn't stop until they were well within the cover of the trees and bushes. It wouldn't stop the shots, but it would make them a more difficult target.

Tucking her behind the thick branches of a low bush, he swept a hand over her head. "Stay here."

Worried eyes flashed up at him. "Where are you going?"

"To find the shooter, lass. Promise me you won't move." When she didn't answer, he gripped her chin, lifting her face. "Promise me, Vangie."

She wanted to be strong, not show the terror coursing through her. "I'll stay here. Please, be careful."

Kissing her, he grinned. "Always."

Eustice finished brushing down the horse before leading it into the corral out back. It had been a long, hot day and the forge had been going most of it. For two hours, while he completed his errands, he'd let it cool down, refiring it after returning.

The time away had been invigorating, a release from the mundane work of forging tools, shoeing horses, and repairing wagon wheels. Eustice rarely took time off. He needed the money from his business to eat, buy essentials, and save.

He had plans. One day, Eustice planned to sell the blacksmith and livery, using the funds to buy a ranch. Near the Circle M would be nice, but he'd purchase what he could afford.

"You're back."

Eustice whirled around at the familiar voice, grabbing a hammer from the nearby workbench. He didn't say a word, staring at the man he never wanted to see again.

"Do you remember me, Eustice?"

Giving a slow nod, he took a step forward. "You need to leave."

"That will not be happening. We've come to speak with the Rousseau woman. She owes us money, and we're here to get it back."

Eustice moved enough to glance behind Reggie, looking for his brother. "Leave her alone."

He ignored the demand. "Where is she?" Reggie already knew where to find her, but Eustice didn't know that.

"I don't know." It was a lie. Eustice knew where she was, and even though he didn't like her being away from town, he understood the reason she'd left.

"Are you certain? Because I'm pretty sure you know exactly where to find her."

Tightening his grip on the hammer, Eustice took a menacing step forward. He wanted to stop this man from hurting Vangie. He'd stop anyone who threatened her, or couldn't protect her.

A growl sounded before Eustice felt his feet moving closer. "Get out."

A nervous chuckle burst from Reggie's throat as he took a couple steps back. For the first time, he realized he misjudged Eustice. The big man might seem simple and affable, but he wouldn't allow himself to be taken.

"Leave. Now." The snarl came out hard and unbending.

Moving to the open front of the livery, Reggie stopped and turned around. "This isn't over."

Eustice watched him leave, his grip on the hammer damp and shaky. The Riordans had to be stopped, and it couldn't come soon enough.

Chapter Twenty-Five

Circle M

"As fast as the shots started, they stopped."

Cam held a glass of whiskey, pacing the study in his aunt's home while the women took care of Vangie and made supper. He'd finished explaining what had happened next to the river.

"I never saw him. Searched, but couldn't find where he hid." Cam rubbed the back of his neck, frustrated and angry.

Colin, Quinn, Fletcher, Bram, and their uncles, Ewan and Ian, sat or stood nearby. With Thane in a bed upstairs, his memory still impaired, and a mystery shooter going after Cam and Vangie, the time had come for a family meeting. They were through being targeted by unknown assailants.

"We should be bringing Brodie and Sam in on this." Colin tossed back his drink. Two of his family were in danger, and he'd come to the end of his patience.

"I'll ride to town and get them." Bram set his empty glass down.

"Nae. Not yet." Ewan, the older of the two surviving uncles, remained calm on the exterior. Underneath, they knew he was as angry as the rest of them. Brodie was his oldest son, Sam was married to his oldest daughter, Jinny. Even if it was their job as lawmen, he had no desire to put them in the crosshairs of a killer.

"Why not?" Colin's brows bunched together.

"It's simple, lad. They'll be bound by laws we can ignore." Standing, Ewan moved across the room, looking out the window into the fading sunlight. "We'll be leaving later tonight for the gypsy camp. All the men and two ranch hands. The rest will stay here to guard the rest of the family. We won't leave until we have answers and the man who's been threatening us."

"What of the women and children in their camp?"

"We'll not be harming them, Bram. We only want those responsible for shooting Thane and trying to kill Cam and Vangie."

"They won't be giving up any of their people, Da." Fletcher had no doubt Belcher Grey and the rest would stand firm. "They'll be hiding them if needed."

Ian spoke for the first time. "They'll not be able to conceal the men forever."

The door to the study slammed open. Audrey stepped inside, her eyes wild as she looked from one man to the next. "It's Thane. He's starting to remember."

Quinn sat on one side of the bed, Bram on the other, their mother next to him. She held Thane's hand, encouraging him to talk when he was ready

227

while Ewan and Ian pressed him with questions. He'd propped himself up so he could see everyone.

Thane blinked several times, as if clearing his head and the memories locked deep inside. Licking his lips, he focused on his mother, her kind eyes urging him to relax and take his time.

"Maybe we should do this another time." Audrey squeezed her son's hand.

"Nae, Ma. I need to let them know what I remember."

Her gaze met Ewan's, who nodded.

Pursing her lips, she sucked in a slow breath, focusing on Thane. "All right, but if you don't feel well, stop."

He didn't speak right away, closing his eyes. "I remember he wore black. Everything was black. His hat, shirt, pants." Thane opened his eyes. "He wore a black tie. And..." His voice trailed off, eyes closing again.

No one spoke, letting him gather his thoughts.

"Even his eyes were black, his skin blotchy and red. He wasn't real tall. Not as tall as most of you. And he was slender."

"Did he wear a coat, lad?" Quinn asked.

"Nae." Swallowing, he reached for a glass of water, Audrey beating him to it. She held it out to him. When finished, he gave it back. "I don't know how far away he was. All I remember is he raised his rifle and shot."

Thane closed his eyes again, sucking in a shaky breath. "That's all I remember."

Quinn placed a hand on his shoulder. "You did good, lad. Now, get some sleep."

"I want to go along when you search for him."

"Nae." Several of them spoke at once, their voices firm.

Ian touched his arm. "You'll be staying here."

"I can help you find him, Uncle Ian."

Audrey looked between her son and uncle. "You're not walking yet, Thane."

He threw off the covers, his face full of determination as he moved one, then the other leg over the side of the bed. Thane had been walking a few steps twice a day with the help of his mother, Quinn, or Bram. No more than eight, no less than three at a time. Each day, he'd become stronger, as well as more anxious to get out of the room and back on his horse.

If he hadn't been shot, Thane knew he'd already be working with his cousin, Blaine, on their ranch up north. Instead, he'd fought for his life, then worked to recover. All because a stranger took pleasure in almost killing him.

That was the way Thane looked at it. Why else would the man shoot a stranger who posed no threat?

Waving away his mother and brothers, he steadied himself on the edge of the bed stand and straightened. Unbeknownst to his family, Thane had been getting up in the middle of the night, walking from the bed to a wall and back. The round trip had increased from one the first night to six last night.

Sweat built on his forehead as he took one step, then another, increasing the pace until his hand met the door. Turning, his gaze locked on the others in the room.

"If you won't let me go with you, I'll be following you."

The men stared at him, glancing at each other before Quinn threw his head back and laughed. "Seems you'll be coming with us, lad."

Jean-Paul rode his horse into camp, bent over from the bullet wound to his side. He'd almost toppled from the saddle several times while covering the distance from the last point he'd seen Turner. Before his *friend* had drawn his gun, shot him, and taken off with the bulk of the money.

It wasn't often Jean-Paul was caught by surprise. He hadn't seen the attack coming. Then again, Turner hadn't expected Jean-Paul to exact revenge so quickly.

Summoning all his strength, the gypsy had drawn his rifle from its scabbard. It was a Sharps rifle used by Union sharpshooters. He'd won it from a cowboy in a card game when the family passed through St. Louis a year ago. Deadly accurate in the right hands.

Using his last scraps of energy, Jean-Paul had locked the butt of the rifle against his shoulder, aimed, and fired. Turner lurched forward in the saddle, then fell off, his boot caught in the stirrup. The horse kept going, dragging its rider through dirt, over rocks, and across low brush. After a while, the boot came loose.

By the time Jean-Paul caught up, Turner was dead. An hour later, exhausted, bleeding, and ready to pass out, he'd recovered the money, leaving the body to whatever animals came along first.

It was now close to midnight, the camp silent except for two guards. One at the north end, the other at the south. Neither acknowledged him as he directed his horse to the widow's wagon. Nobody stirred as he slid from the saddle and passed out a couple feet from the steps.

Eyes opening to slits, Jean-Paul groaned in agony. His body was on fire, the pain in his side excruciating. Above him, Belcher's solemn face stared down, his eyes focused and remote. A cold cloth lay across his forehead.

He didn't look down. By now, the woman who functioned as their doctor would've cleaned and dressed the wound, stuffing it with a special poultice to defend against infection. When he tried to lift a hand to his face, he stilled. His right hand was secured to a metal rod by leather straps. His left hand remained free.

Opening his mouth to protest, he choked, lungs burning, eyes watering. Moving his free hand to his mouth, Jean-Paul continued to cough, his face paling to a ghostly white.

"Drink this." Belcher lifted his head, holding a dented tin cup to his mouth, urging Jean-Paul to take a sip. "It's whiskey. It will help with the pain."

Parting his lips, he took a couple sips, then closed his eyes on another cough. Feeling Belcher lay his head back onto the pillow, exhaustion overtook him.

When he woke again, sunlight streamed through a slit in the thin, cotton curtains. Belcher was gone, but another of the men sat a foot away. If possible, he was less affable about tending him than Belcher. It didn't take long for Jean-Paul to drift off to sleep again.

The next time he woke, it was to the sounds of loud voices. He recognized some, but not others. Jean-Paul tried to sit up, but failed, falling back onto the bed.

His side throbbed, as did his head. He wanted to get up, move around, stretch his back, and feel alive.

The loud voices outside changed to shouts. Belcher's became one of the loudest. Jean-Paul could make out the words, recognizing the Scottish lilt of the MacLarens.

Stomach clenching, fear gripped him. Ignoring the pain, Jean-Paul forced himself up, almost passing out from the pain. For the first time, he looked at the wound in his side and grimaced.

The bandage was soaked through, red with his blood. It surprised him. He wondered how long it had been since the woman had tended to it. She was dedicated to her job of doctoring the family, her medical skills more than adequate. What he saw indicated she hadn't been to see him in hours.

He looked around for a clean shirt, grabbing one from a nearby hook on the wall. Gritting his teeth, Jean-Paul slipped his arms into it, then stood, almost collapsing back onto the bed at the pain. Bracing himself against a wall, he sucked in a ragged breath.

No matter the pain, he had to get away. They'd never believe he hadn't meant to shoot the kid. But the voices in his head had told him to shoot, made him lift the rifle and fire. When he'd seen the blood, Jean-Paul panicked, ran back to his horse, and ridden south. But the voices in his head didn't stop.

They'd haunted him more often, talking to him, telling him what to do. He'd tried to fight them, turning to alcohol to still the voices. It worked for a while.

When whiskey no longer worked, he visited a store in Chinatown. In the back, behind a wall of thick curtains, was an opium den. Areas were sectioned off so customers would have privacy while they smoked.

The opium gave Jean-Paul instant relief. He'd returned several times, always leaving by a private door in back. Every visit provided respite from the voices and their insistent orders.

The day he'd returned to camp and saw the boy watching, there'd been no opium to quell the voices. The shooting hadn't been his fault, but they'd never believe him.

Shaky fingers closed the buttons on his shirt. Picking up his pants off the floor, he sat down, slipping his legs inside before lifting socks out of his boots.

The shouting outside continued, his fear growing. Feeling weak, he forced himself to stand again, sick and dizzy.

Securing his gunbelt around his waist and picking up his hat, he moved to the front of the wagon, stepping through a small opening. Blinking several times, he looked around, heart pounding in his chest. The voices came from the back of the wagon. Not as loud, but he could still make them out.

Lifting one leg, then the other over the threshold, he stilled, wild eyes scanning the camp. Taking in a steadying breath, he bent over at the pain ripping through him. He could already see blood seeping through his shirt.

If he left, he might bleed to death. If he stayed, they would hang him. Shoulders sagging, Jean-Paul made the only choice he could.

Ignoring the piercing sensation in his side, he climbed to the ground. Taking several steps, he moved toward the back of the camp, wanting to reach the cover of the trees before anyone spotted him.

The sound of a six-shooter being cocked stopped his progress.

Colin took a couple steps closer. "Raise your hands and turn around. You'll be leaving with us, lad."

Chapter Twenty-Six

Cam stood behind Colin. Bram and Fletcher positioned themselves on either side of him, standing guard, making certain he didn't rush forward to attack the man. Belcher had called him Jean-Paul.

"It's him." Thane's strained voice had them turning to look at him. He stood on the other side of Bram, Uncle Ewan next to him, helping his nephew stand.

"You're certain, lad?" Cam asked.

"Aye."

Cam stared at the man who shot Thane and tried to kill him and Vangie. "Where will we be taking him, Colin?"

"I'm not going anywhere with you." Jean-Paul took a step away, his voice indignant. "I've done nothing."

Ewan assisted Thane when he started to move forward. "You shot me."

A flash of recognition showed in the gypsy's eyes, but he didn't respond.

"You almost killed me." Thane tried to get close. Ewan and Bram stopped him.

Body beginning to tremble, Jean-Paul clamped his broad hands over his head, squeezing. "I can't think." Bending at the waist, he dropped to the ground, crying out at the pain in his side. "They won't stop."

Belcher hurried up to him, kneeling beside Jean-Paul. He settled a hand on his shoulder. "You need to have your wound checked."

Shaking his head, he reared back, roaring in agony. His hands pushed harder against his head as he rocked back and forth.

"They won't leave me alone," he erupted, his eyes wide and wild.

Belcher rubbed his back, trying to calm him. Reaching into a pocket, he pulled out a flask and opened it. "Drink this, Jean-Paul."

Grabbing it out of Belcher's hand, he tipped it back, finishing what was left. Swiping a sleeve across his mouth, he handed it back.

"What's wrong with the lad?" Colin asked.

Belcher continued to rub Jean-Paul's back, his expression grim. "He isn't right in the head. Started a few years ago." Letting out a ragged breath, he slowly shook his head. "He hears voices. They tell him what to do."

Cam watched Jean-Paul rock himself, a low keening sounding through his lips. "Voices?"

"That's what he calls them. He doesn't have them all the time, but it has been getting worse over the last year." Belcher pulled back Jean-Paul's shirt. "We need to get him inside or he'll bleed to death."

237

Colin cast a quick glance at Cam, seeing the same thought on his brother's face. Neither believed it would be a huge loss if the man bled out. But it wasn't in their nature to let it happen.

They helped get Jean-Paul on his feet, then lifted him into their arms. Getting him back into the wagon the same way he came out wasn't possible. He had to be carried up the steps and inside.

After setting him back onto the bed, a middle-aged woman joined them. She carried a basket filled with what appeared to be medicines, potions, and bandages. Motioning for everyone to leave the wagon, she got to work.

The MacLarens gathered together several feet away, talking in low voices about what Belcher had told them.

"Do you believe him, Colin?" Fletcher asked.

"I've no idea what to believe. Hearing voices?" He rested fisted hands on his hips, his attention moving to the back of the wagon. "We need to get Brodie and one of the doctors."

"I'll go." Fletcher didn't wait for an answer before hurrying to his horse.

"I'm coming with you, lad." Bram grabbed the reins to Bullet and swung into the saddle.

They reined toward the main trail, riding as fast as possible over the winding path toward town. It didn't take long to reach the eastern boundary.

Fletcher continued to the jail while Bram headed toward the clinic.

Dismounting, Bram shoved the door open. "Is anyone here?"

Jonathan Vickery walked out of one of the examination rooms. "Bram."

Accepting the doctor's outstretched hand, Bram studied the man a moment longer than necessary. It was the first time he'd seen the doctor since Cam had mentioned he may have an interest in Bram's mother, Audrey. Releasing his grip, he stepped away.

"Can you come with Fletcher and me to the gypsy camp?"

"Why?"

"A man's been shot and they can't stop the bleeding." Bram looked down, shoving his hands into his pockets. "There's something else."

Waiting, Vickery cocked his head.

"The lad says he hears voices. Voices that make him do stuff."

"What kind of stuff?"

Uneasy with something he didn't understand, Bram's lips drew into a thin line. It sounded crazy, but the doc needed to know.

"From what we heard, they told him to shoot someone at least once."

Vickery moved back toward the exam room, going straight to a bookcase on one wall. Pulling out a thick volume, he thumbed through it, read a moment, thumbed a few more pages and read some more. Closing the book, he set it back on the shelf.

"Let me get my bag."

"What's wrong with him, Doc?"

"I'm not certain. At least not yet. I'll get my horse ready."

"Fletcher went to get Brodie. We'll meet you at the jail."

Brodie and Sam joined them for the ride back to the camp. Fletcher had told them the same information Bram had shared with Vickery. They'd looked at him as if he were daft, but didn't hesitate to grab their horses and follow.

As they got closer to the camp, Brodie sidled up to Fletcher. "Has he admitted to anything?"

"Nae. He spoke of voices telling him to do something, but never admitted to shooting Thane."

"What about trying to kill Cam and Vangie?"

"We didn't get that far before Colin wanted us to come for you and the doctor. He has to be guilty, including robbing the bank. Nothing else makes sense."

Brodie didn't respond. He thought the same, but it would be a judge and jury who'd decide the man's innocence or guilt. What they needed to do was keep him alive long enough to stand trial.

Reaching the camp, Vickery dismounted, grabbing his bag before rushing toward Colin and the other MacLarens.

"The lad's in the wagon, Doc." Before Colin could start up the steps, a tall, burly man moved to block them.

"We have our own doctor."

Vickery held out his hand. "I'm Jonathan Vickery, one of the doctors in Conviction. I've considerable experience with gunshot wounds. Perhaps I can assist your doctor."

The man crossed his arms, planting his feet shoulder width apart. "She doesn't need your help."

"Why don't you let me go inside and see for myself?"

The door to the wagon opened, Belcher staring down at them. "Let the doctor inside."

A disgruntled expression twisted the man's face, but he moved aside.

Vickery took the steps, entering the wagon. Belcher closed the door, indicating no one else would be welcome. Brodie ignored the warning.

Bounding up the steps, he shoved the door open, entering before anyone could protest. Belcher's shocked expression was almost comical.

"You are not welcome here."

"As soon as Doc Vickery determines his condition, I'll be taking the lad to jail."

"He's done nothing." Belcher had no intention of letting Jean-Paul be taken from the camp.

"A judge will decide that. Not you or anyone else. I'll not be leaving here without him." Brodie noticed Vickery kneeling next to Jean-Paul, opening his satchel. The woman had moved aside to give him room. A good sign.

Vickery looked over his shoulder at them. "Both of you should leave while we tend to the patient. The wagon is too small for this many people."

"Call out if you need me, Doc."

"I will, Sheriff."

Belcher sat on a bench, unwilling to leave. Brodie wouldn't allow the older man to go against Vickery's orders.

"We'll be doing what the doctor wants." He shoved the door open, motioning for Belcher to precede him outside.

When Belcher didn't move, Brodie grabbed him by the collar, jerking him up. "We've no time for this." He shoved him toward the open doorway, not letting go until Belcher took the steps to the ground. Brodie followed him outside.

"Sam, make sure he doesn't go back inside before Vickery says it's all right."

Taking Belcher's arm, Sam guided him away from the wagon toward a group of gypsies. Their faces showed disgust at having outsiders take over their camp.

Sam didn't care what any of them thought. They were trying to protect a man who'd almost killed Thane, robbed the bank, and shot at Cam and Vangie. He would go to jail, face trial, and spend years in prison.

Letting go of Belcher's arm, Sam rested his hand on the handle of his six-shooter. Quinn and Bram came up beside him in a show of support.

Sam looked at the group of men, then at Belcher. "Don't interfere. There's no reason for any of the rest of you to go to jail."

He could tell they wanted to protest, but held their tongues. If any of them tried to help Jean-Paul escape, they'd be dealing with a group of MacLaren men determined to stop them. Sam might not be a MacLaren, but he was married to one, and they protected their own, the same as the gypsies.

Grousing among themselves, the group turned away.

Two hours passed before Vickery left the wagon. His movements and lines on his face showed fatigue and something else. When he reached the ground, his gaze locked on Brodie as he walked toward him.

"Did the lad talk to you, Doc?"

Vickery lowered himself onto a nearby log, placing his satchel on the ground. Scrubbing both hands over his face, he leaned back, his attention going back to the wagon.

"He's a sick man, Brodie."

"From the wound?"

"He'll recover from the gunshot. It's his mind that may never heal."

Brodie sat next to him, shooting a warning glance at Belcher when he began to walk toward them. The glare stopped him before Sam had a chance to block his path.

"Jean-Paul didn't talk much, but what he did say isn't comforting. He repeated over and over how he didn't hurt anyone. Something about the voices ordering him to do things he didn't want to do."

"What does it mean, Doc?"

"I've no doubt he shot Thane and robbed the bank. The problem is his mind is gone, Brodie. I'll need more time with him after he recovers to give you a complete medical opinion."

"Are you saying the lad isn't responsible for what he's done?"

"He's responsible, but does he belong in prison or an asylum? I won't be able to tell you until I've asked him more questions."

Brodie nodded, understanding he could do nothing except move Jean-Paul to the jail. He and his deputies would keep him fed and make sure he had medical care.

"Did he admit to shooting at Cam and Vangie?"

"I didn't get a chance to ask before he passed out." Vickery rubbed his brow, letting out a long, ragged breath. "My gut tells me he's not the one."

"How could he not be?"

Vickery thought a minute before answering. "If the voices in Jean-Paul's head had told him to hunt them, they'd be dead."

Chapter Twenty-Seven

Conviction

Reggie and Merle sat at a table at Buckie's Castle, glasses and a bottle of whiskey between them. Earlier, they'd stood on the boardwalk with many others, watching Brodie, Sam, and Doc Vickery return with a man in the back of a wagon. Rumors circulated within minutes of them moving the man into the jail.

He was the one who'd robbed the bank. He'd been the man to shoot the MacLaren boy.

There were others, but those two were the most common. The Riordans didn't care about the man or what he'd done. Their minds were on Eustice.

It had taken Reggie almost the entire night before to talk Merle into doing what was necessary. His brother had been obstinate. He wanted to set up a meeting with Vangie, tell her what her father had done, and ask for their money back.

By now, Eustice had probably told her they were in town. Merle saw no reason to hide any longer. Be direct, obtain the funds, head home...and not use Eustice as leverage. He'd lost the argument.

Before they'd fallen asleep, Reggie had turned him to his way of thinking. It had come after a promise they wouldn't hurt Eustice or Vangie. It was a promise Reggie would try to keep.

Tossing back his second whiskey, Merle talked through what they'd decided. They'd visit Eustice at his apartment before he went down to the livery tomorrow morning.

They'd purchased clothes common to local ranchers. Blending in would be important if anyone saw them enter the livery. The Riordans would look the same as any of the dozens of cowboys around Conviction.

Eustice wouldn't be moved from his apartment. Instead, he'd be bound and gagged. If anyone came looking, they'd get no answer to their knocks and shouts.

Reggie had already identified a young boy they'd pay to deliver the message to Circle M. It wouldn't be threatening. They'd simply tell her Eustice needed to see her.

The message would explain he was sick and hadn't been able to open the livery. She'd be worried enough to ride in from the MacLaren ranch, check his condition for herself.

There'd be no bullying, blackmail, or extortion. Just a clear understanding Vangie owed them money and they expected to be paid. It would be a business transaction. They'd get their money, sign a document saying "paid in full", and leave town. The law couldn't come after them for being paid money owed.

"Are we doing this in the morning?" Merle filled another glass, sipping instead of tossing it back.

"It will do no good to wait. Evangeline might not return to town for days, and I don't plan to stay longer than necessary."

"Good. I want to get this over with." Draining the glass, Merle set it on the scarred, wood table. "I'm going to the Gold Dust for supper."

Drinking the last of his whiskey, Reggie stood. "I'll go with you. When we're finished, we'll prepare for our early morning visit to Eustice."

Circle M

A couple hours after sunup, Vangie helped Kyla hang the damp clothes on the line out back. They'd been talking about her upcoming wedding to August. It would take place at the ranch in less than a month, yet Kyla didn't seem at all nervous. Or excited.

Her demeanor didn't change whether they spoke of work around the ranch or getting married a second time.

"Mr. Fielder is such a wonderful man, Kyla. You're quite fortunate."

Attaching a blouse to the line with a clothespin, she let her arms drop to her sides, a wistful expression on her face. "Aye, he is a good man. I respect him a great deal."

Pursing her lips, Vangie considered the question she'd wanted to ask since arriving at the ranch. It wasn't her place to pry. Once she and Cam were married, Vangie might feel more comfortable expressing her thoughts.

"You've been wondering if I love him, haven't you, lass?"

Vangie let the shirt she held drop back into the basket. "Well, yes."

"I've been asking myself the same." Grabbing the shirt Vangie had dropped, Kyla shook it before attaching it to the line with two clothespins. "Angus will always own my heart, lass. I fell in love with him when he was a young lad and the love never wavered. Since his death, I've been living each day as if I were also dead."

She picked up another shirt, holding the damp fabric in both hands. "August makes me feel alive. He cares a great deal about me and the family, and I respect him."

"Do you like him?" Vangie shook out a heavy pair of pants.

"Aye. But I don't love him. Maybe someday..." Kyla shrugged, resigned to never again feel the deep love she and Angus had shared. "Do you love my son?"

The question caught Vangie unaware, her hands shaking as she pinned the pants to the line. She wondered if Cam had told his mother about his proposal and her acceptance. They'd agreed to say nothing until after Kyla and August's wedding, not wanting to take away their joy.

"Yes, I do. Very much."

Kyla nodded, a small smile lifting the corners of her mouth. "The lad feels the same. Has he asked you to marry him?"

Vangie thought of their promise, wondering how angry he'd get if his mother knew.

"I can see on your face he has. Did you accept?"

She captured her lower lip between her teeth, then smiled. "Yes, I accepted."

Kyla threw up her hands. "That's wonderful news, lass!" Grasping Vangie in a hug, she kissed her cheek before letting go.

"We weren't going to say anything until after your wedding."

"Nonsense. You'll not be waiting any longer. They'll all be so happy for you and Cam. We'll be planning a celebration supper."

Kyla's enthusiasm had Vangie laughing, joyful tears forming in her eyes. She realized how much Cam's happiness meant to his mother, how much it would mean to all the MacLarens.

"This Saturday when Brodie, Maggie, Sam, and Jinny are able to ride out from town."

"And August," Vangie added.

A blush crept up Kyla's face. "Aye. August, too."

The sound of an approaching rider turned their attention to the road from town. They'd begun to relax after Jean-Paul's arrest. Still, they tensed at the sight of a lone boy atop a large buckskin with black points.

"That gelding belongs to Eustice." The words came out of Vangie's mouth without thought. "He's the only one who rides him."

Waving, the boy stopped several feet away. "I have a message for Miss Evangeline Rousseau." He reached into his pocket, pulling out a piece of paper.

Vangie stepped forward. "I'm Miss Rousseau."

Relief washed over the boy's face. "This is for you."

She took the paper from his hand. Opening it, she read the words, then read them again and looked up. "Did you see Eustice?"

"He's the blacksmith, right?"

"Yes."

"No. Another man paid me to get this to you. He came out of the livery and waved at me." The boy smiled. "Gave me a full dollar and told me to ride this horse. It's the best day I've had in a long time."

Vangie handed the note to Kyla. "I need to saddle Duchess and go to him."

"Not alone, lass."

"There's no one here. All the men are out with the herd."

"I'll wait and ride back to town with you, ma'am."

Acknowledging the boy's offer, Vangie headed to the barn to saddle her mare.

"What's your name, lad?" Kyla asked.

"William, but everyone calls me Billy."

Kyla moved next to the buckskin. "Did you recognize the man who gave you the note?"

"No. He looked the same as all the other cowboys around town."

She glanced at the barn, then back at Billy. "You'll be riding back to town with Miss Rousseau. All the way to the livery."

"Yes, ma'am."

"Then you'll be getting the sheriff. Do you know Brodie MacLaren?"

"Everybody knows him."

"Aye. Tell him Aunt Kyla wants him to check on Eustice. Do you understand, lad?"

"Sure, but Miss Rousseau will already be with the blacksmith."

"True, but I'm wanting the sheriff to check on him also."

Billy grew silent, waiting while Vangie saddled her horse. When she rode out of the barn, he gave Kyla a grave look. "Do you think something is wrong?"

"I don't know, lad. That's why I'm wanting Brodie to check on Eustice."

"Yes, ma'am. I'll be sure to get him."

Kyla watched them ride off, a burning sense of dread building in her chest. As Vangie said, the family and ranch hands were with the herd. They weren't expected back until later in the day. She'd have to trust Billy would send Brodie to the livery. It was the best Kyla could do until Cam returned.

Conviction

Merle sat on an old sofa in the sparse, but clean apartment above the blacksmith shop. Reggie stood across the room, looking out a window toward the street. Eustice sat a few feet away, his wrists tied to the arms of an old wooden chair.

The gag had been removed after Reggie sent the boy to Circle M. Even if Eustice shouted, no one could hear him. Not with the bustling street and noises from the riverfront less than a block away.

"Vangie doesn't have money to give you," Eustice said in a calm, even voice.

Reggie turned away from the window, a smirk on his face. "She's got plenty of money."

"What she has belongs to her, not you."

Crossing his arms, Reggie leaned against the wall. "Her father owes it."

"He's dead."

"Doesn't matter. His debt passes to her."

Eustice blinked a couple times as he thought over the statement. It made no sense to him. "I think you're lying. When he died, you lost your money. Whatever she has is hers, not yours."

Merle leaned back in the sofa, listening to the exchange. Eustice's mind was simple, but what he said made sense. No judge would uphold the claim when it had never been written down and signed. They couldn't even prove the debt was owed. Reggie relied on intimidation and harassment to get his way.

It surprised Merle how calm his brother had been from the time they'd burst into the apartment. He hadn't raised his voice or made any threats. Definitely not Reggie's usual approach. Standing, he walked into the tiny kitchen.

"I'll tell Vangie not to pay you anything."

Chuckling, Reggie shook his head. "She'll pay it. Miss Rousseau will do whatever is needed to keep you safe."

Eustice thought about it, knowing Reggie was right. Vangie would do all she could to protect him, the same as he'd do for her. The same as he'd been doing for her for years.

Reggie walked closer, lowering his voice. "And if you say anything to stop her, I'll tell her what I know."

Eustice stared at him, eyes wide. "About what?"

A knowing gleam shown in Reggie's gaze. "You aren't the only one watching over her."

Chapter Twenty-Eight

Billy rode beside Vangie, making good time back to town. He'd seen the concern in her eyes, as well as in Mrs. MacLaren's, and wondered what was happening. At fifteen, Billy had been on his own long enough to know when something wasn't right.

The MacLarens were important people in Conviction, one of the richest families in the region. He'd heard one of the older women would be marrying August Fielder, but he didn't know which one. It didn't matter. Fielder was another prominent man, the president of the Bank of Conviction, an attorney who'd recently been appointed as a judge.

Anything involving those families was important. If he did a good job, maybe he could get a job at the ranch, or work for Fielder.

Approaching the boundary of town, he took the street toward the livery. They stopped outside the closed door to the blacksmith shop, Vangie noting the sign saying it was closed.

They dismounted, Billy running to the gate of the livery to let them in.

"Thank you, Billy. I can go up alone."

"If you don't mind, I'll be going with you, ma'am."

She didn't respond when he followed her up the outside steps to the door of the apartment. Vangie didn't bother to knock, just turned the knob. Opening it, her mouth dropped open an instant before she shrieked.

Billy tried to grab her arm, but someone hauled her inside and slammed the door shut. Knowing he could do nothing by himself, he rushed down the steps, ran to the front, and mounted the buckskin.

Kicking the horse's sides, he rode straight to the sheriff's office, dismounted, and hurried inside. One of the deputies stood next to the stove, sipping from a tin cup.

"I need to find Sheriff Brodie."

"He's busy in back. What do you need?" Sam's gaze wandered over the boy, recognizing him as one of several who made their living any way they could.

"It's important. I think someone is hurting Miss Evangeline."

Setting down the cup, Sam stepped toward him. "Where is she?" The last he knew, she was still at Circle M.

"Mr. Eustice's apartment."

"Are you certain? I don't believe Eustice would ever hurt her."

"Not him. It's the other men inside with them."

His mind went to the Riordan brothers, the men he'd heard were after Vangie for money her father was accused of owing.

"Stay here." Sam hurried to the back. A moment later, he returned with Brodie.

"What is this about Vangie, lad?"

Billy stared at the sheriff, his throat working. "I think someone may be trying to hurt her. She's in the apartment above the blacksmith shop. There are two men in there with her and Eustice."

Cursing, Brodie grabbed his hat and ran outside, Sam and Billy right behind him. They hurried past Seth, who joined them, asking no questions.

They were only two blocks from the livery. Brodie hoped they were close enough.

Circle M

"When are you going ask the lass to marry you, lad?" Colin rode next to Cam on their way home. Quinn, Fletcher, and Bram were close behind, waiting for Cam's response.

They'd finished their work with the herd early, leaving the ranch hands to watch over the animals. The MacLarens were anxious to get back to the ranch, make certain nothing else had happened since they'd left that morning.

Each day brought something new, but it had been a while since they'd faced unresolved threats. The arrest of Jean-Paul provided some respite. They knew he'd shot Thane and robbed the bank, certain he was the one who'd tried to kill Cam and Vangie.

Those crimes didn't solve the mystery of the Riordan brothers. Eustice swore he saw them, but no matter how much Brodie and his men searched, they hadn't been able to spot them. Maybe they were worried about men who didn't exist, or who wouldn't be coming for Vangie.

Cam kept his gaze on the trail ahead, not answering Colin's question. He and Vangie had made a promise to keep their betrothal secret until after his mother's wedding to August.

"You are going to ask the lass, aren't you?"

A smile spread across Cam's face. "Aye. I'll be asking her." Warmth spread through him, the same as it did each time he thought of Vangie.

"You'd better be hurrying, Cam," Quinn called from behind them. "You're not the only lad interested in her."

He'd love to wipe the grin from his cousin's face by telling him the truth, but he'd agreed to stay silent, and he would. "Vangie's only wanting me. Of that I'm sure."

"Cocky eejit, aren't you?" Fletcher said, but there was humor in his voice.

"It's not cocky when it's true," Cam shot back.

They continued their banter all the way to the ranch. Riding toward the barn, the group reined around when Kyla ran from the house, waving her arms. A stab of fear pierced Cam at the angst on his mother's face.

"What is it, Ma?" He slid to the ground, as did Colin.

"It's Vangie. She's gone to town."

"Why?" Cam asked, glancing over his shoulder toward the trail to Conviction.

"Eustice sent a lad with a note saying he needed her."

"What lad?" Colin asked.

"His name is Billy. He said a man gave him the note, not Eustice. He rode with her back to town." She pressed a hand to her stomach, her lips thin and pale. "I'm not feeling right about it."

Without discussion, Cam and Colin swung back atop their horses, reining them toward town. Bram, Quinn, and Fletcher rode right behind them, not one questioning the decision to find her.

Conviction

"We aren't leaving until you agree to give us the money your father owes us." Reggie kept his voice low, calm, knowing they could wait Vangie out. They weren't going anywhere until they had the money. It didn't matter if it took an hour or a week. He and

Merle were willing to wait it out. At least Reggie was. He wasn't as certain about his brother.

"I must apologize, Mr. Riordan, but I have no idea what money you're talking about. My father is dead, and I found no evidence of a debt to you and your brother." Vangie's response was as calm as Reggie's request. She had no intention of allowing herself to be intimidated.

"You can't tell me Eustice didn't mention we tried to find you in Grand Rapids, Evangeline."

"I'm not denying it, Reggie. What I am questioning is your legal right to demand payment of a debt when there's no record of one. If you have any hope of obtaining the funds, you'll need to provide legal evidence."

Reggie glanced at Merle, who stayed silent. His brother had confronted him about the same, saying their case would never be approved by a judge without a signed note. That was why Reggie planned to use subtle intimidation without threatening the woman.

From what he'd learned, Evangeline Rousseau was a timid, bookish woman who would bend to their demand. So far, he'd seen none of what he expected. Instead, she was calm and firm, not the retiring person he'd been led to believe.

"I have proof, but not with me. Regardless, the money is owed." He looked at Merle. "Tell her."

Not for the first time, Merle heard the lie in his brother's voice. And the slightest bit of desperation.

He'd seen it before. Reggie would start calm, becoming impatient, then violent when he didn't get what he wanted.

The Rousseau woman posed a problem from the moment Reggie had dragged her inside. She'd recovered well from the initial surprise of seeing Eustice tied to a chair. Her first response had been to demand they release him.

At first, they'd offered condescending smiles before their features grew serious at the determined look on her face. They were up against a much more formidable woman than anticipated.

"I won't be intimidated into handing over money. Either you have the proof or you don't. Either way, you'll be dealing with my attorney, August Fielder. I trust you've heard of him."

By the expressions on their faces, indeed they had. Vangie saw the instant Reggie changed. His features hardened, jaw muscles clenching, face reddening in building rage.

"You're making a mistake, Miss Rousseau," he ground out, taking a menacing step forward.

She didn't budge from her position next to Eustice. "You're the one making a mistake if you believe you can hurt either one of us and get out of town. The sheriff, as well as the entire MacLaren family, will hunt you down. Depending on their mood, you may or may not live to stand trial."

It was all bluster. Vangie had no idea what Brodie or the rest of the MacLarens would do, but Reggie and Merle didn't know that.

"Not if we take you with us. We may not get the money, but we will get the satisfaction of seeing both of you suffer." Reggie moved forward, gripping one of her arms and wrenching it behind her. "Get me the length of leather, Merle. And the gag."

Merle hesitated, having no desire to hurt Vangie or Eustice. "We should leave. We'll return when you find the documents proving the debt." Documents Merle knew didn't exist.

Dragging Vangie across the room with him, he backhanded Merle across the face. "Get the tie."

Stunned into action, Merle reached into his pocket, pulling out the leather thong. Reggie grasped Vangie's other arm, holding both behind her.

"Tie her up." Reggie reached into his own pocket, removing a bandanna and stuffing it into her mouth. "And hurry up. We need to get them both out of here before anyone comes to check on Eustice."

The words had just left his mouth when someone pounded on the door. Reggie whipped Vangie in front of him, but not before Eustice shouted out.

"They have Vangie!"

Reggie had no time to react before the door burst open. Brodie, Sam, and Seth rushed inside, their guns in front of them.

"Let her go!" Brodie shouted, moving so he had a clean shot at Reggie's head.

At the same time, Sam trained his gun on Merle while Seth untied Eustice.

Merle held up his arms, surrendering. Reggie did the opposite, a fierce expression of contempt on his face. Dragging Vangie backward, he reached down, withdrawing his gun from its holster, holding it to her temple.

"You're going to back away and let us walk out of here."

"Don't be stupid, Reggie. Let her go." There was a pleading tone in Merle's voice, but his brother ignored it.

"Listen to him," Brodie said. "You won't make it out of here."

"Then neither will she." He shoved the barrel against her temple, causing her to wince in pain.

Instead of moving aside, Brodie, Sam, and Seth formed a wall, blocking the door. The only way of escape.

"We'll not be letting you out of here with Vangie." Brodie saw Seth move a little to the side, knowing his deputy sought an unobstructed aim at Riordan's head.

"Move out of our way." Reggie tried to shove Vangie forward, but she dug in her heels. Then he made a critical mistake. He pulled the gun away and slammed it against her head.

It was the split second Seth needed.

Chapter Twenty-Nine

Cam never slowed his pace, pushing Duke into a gallop toward town. Colin, Quinn, Bram, and Fletcher did the same, their minds on Vangie and what might be happening to her and Eustice.

Reaching the edge of town, none of them slowed, racing down the main street while dodging wagons and pedestrians. Some shouted at them, others glared, but all jumped out of their way.

Cam didn't consider stopping at the jail. His goal was the blacksmith shop and the apartment upstairs. Twenty yards before the front door, he slowed Duke but didn't wait for the palomino gelding to stop before jumping down and running through the livery and up the stairs.

Drawing his gun, Cam kicked the door open and froze. The front room was empty, as was the kitchen.

"Vangie!" he shouted, but no one answered. He moved back to the front room, about ready to shout again when he saw the others staring at a spot on the wall. Blood.

He started for the door, stopping when Colin grabbed his arm. "Where are you going?"

Cam ripped out of his brother's hold. "To find Vangie."

"Then we go to the jail. We need to be speaking with Brodie."

Giving a quick nod, Cam hurried down the stairs, swinging up on Duke and racing back the direction they'd come. He didn't have to look to know his family followed.

Heart pounding, he tried to calm his breathing, finding it impossible. Had it been yesterday he'd asked Vangie to marry him and she'd agreed? He couldn't remember.

He dismounted in front of the jail moments before the others. Colin caught up with him as he opened the door. Deputy Alex Campbell sat at Brodie's desk, a cup of coffee before him.

"Where's Brodie?" Cam stepped closer, his gaze moving quickly around the room.

"The sheriff is at Bay's house." Alex began to stand, stopping midway when Cam and Colin turned, rushing out the door. "Vangie is all right, Cam," he shouted, but no one heard him.

Suzette sat next to Vangie, holding her friend's hand while studying her pale face. Blood stained her clothes and colored her hands, one side of her face, and hair. Bay was upstairs preparing a warm bath.

Vangie had said little since Brodie escorted her and Eustice to the house. Sam had taken Merle to jail while Seth fetched one of the doctors to confirm what they already knew. Reggie hadn't survived the shot from Seth's gun.

Brodie stood a few feet away from the women. It would be a while before Vangie could give her account of what happened. He'd already spoken with Eustice, who'd confirmed the two men were the brothers who'd confronted him in Grand Rapids. Reggie and Merle Riordan. One dead. The other sure to stand trial for crimes Brodie had yet to determine.

A loud knock drew his attention, but Brodie didn't reach the door before it flew open. Cam, Colin, Quinn, Fletcher, and Bram walked in without invitation. Seeing Vangie next to Suzette, Cam rushed forward, kneeling in front of her.

"Vangie?" He threaded his fingers through hers. It took a moment before he noticed the blood on her clothes, splatters on her hands and face. "Vangie. I'm here, lass."

"Cam?"

His name on her lips provided a slight moment of relief. "Aye, lass."

Tears began to well in her eyes. "Cam..."

Wrapping his arms around her, he dragged Vangie forward. Resting her head on his shoulder, quiet sobs shook her trembling frame. Cam rubbed her back, talking in low tones, providing reassurances. Several feet away, Colin and the others walked up to Brodie.

"How'd you hear?" Brodie asked.

Colin's gaze shifted away from Cam and Vangie. "Ma told us a rider arrived with a note saying Eustice needed her. We didn't spend time talking about it before Cam took off to town. The lads and I followed. What happened?"

"Eustice said the Riordans were trying to get Vangie to pay them money her father owed them. Vangie told them she wanted proof. They didn't have any. Seems Reggie got angry and planned to take her. That's when Seth, Sam, and I got there."

Bay, coming down the stairs, interrupted further conversation. "Her bath is ready."

Pulling from their embrace, Cam used a finger to raise her gaze to meet his. "I'll be carrying you upstairs so you can get out of these clothes and wash."

"I can walk."

"I know, lass. But I'm still going to carry you." Slipping his arms underneath her legs and back, Cam lifted Vangie against his chest and climbed the stairs.

Eustice, Vangie, and almost all the MacLarens sat near the front of the room used for trials, awaiting the verdict. August had called the trial within days of Reggie's death and Merle's arrest. The older brother had been buried in the town's cemetery. They expected Merle to spend years in San Quentin for intended kidnapping, extortion, threatening a lawman, and a few other lesser crimes.

Although Vangie and Eustice testified he'd tried to calm Reggie down, they didn't believe August and the jury would be swayed.

When the jury returned, no one was surprised at the guilty verdicts for each crime. Merle lowered his head into his hands and cried. Deep, wracking sobs from a man who had no intention of hurting Vangie and Eustice. His main crime had been to stick with his brother even when everything began to fall apart.

Cam and Vangie continued to sit there after Merle had been escorted out and everyone else had left. Several minutes passed before Cam rested an arm over her shoulders, drawing her close.

"Are you all right, lass?"

Letting out a short, ragged breath, she nodded. "I'm fine. Glad it's over. Although I do feel bad for Merle."

"The lad made his choices, lass. He could've left and returned home, but chose to stay in Conviction."

"I know you're right. It's just..." Her voice trailed off before she shook her head. "Can we go home now?"

Home.

The one word sent waves of warmth through Cam. They'd announced their betrothal before the trial. There'd been a celebratory supper, lots of toasts, and even more hugs.

August and his mother would be married in two weeks. A month later, he and Vangie would say their vows. Until then, she'd be staying at the ranch, protected and loved.

"Aye, love. We'll be going home."

Eustice stood under the cover of the boardwalk, across the street from where the trial had been held, feeling a crack in the area of his heart. Cam and Vangie stepped outside, holding hands, smiling as they headed toward their wagon. They'd be leaving for the ranch, and in a few weeks, he'd watch them marry. Another fissure to his heart speared his chest.

He'd loved Vangie since they were children. After his accident, and even with his diminished mental capacity, he'd understood they'd never be together. Still, he'd watched over her, deflected bullies, defended any slights by cruel children.

Eustice knew nobody would ever be able to protect Vangie as well as him. Which was why he'd found it necessary to prove it.

No one would ever know Eustice had been the one to fire the shots at her and Cam. Not to kill, but to prove a point. She was precious and loved, and not only by Cam MacLaren.

Vangie would always be the woman he loved, the one person he'd lay down his life to save. And no matter what happened, he would always be there for her.

Epilogue

Circle M
Two weeks later...

Cam kept Vangie close during his mother's wedding to August, and afterward when the party started. Memories of her ordeal with the Riordans would lessen with time. In a month, he and Vangie would be married and start their own life together. He wished it was sooner.

Brushing a kiss across her forehead, he turned at the sight of Brodie approaching with his wife, Maggie, and their son, Shaun. Right behind them were Sam and his wife, Jinny, Brodie's sister.

"You're next, lad." Brodie clasped his cousin's shoulder.

Cam offered a wide grin before looking at Vangie. "Aye, and I couldn't be happier about it."

A few minutes later, the women moved several feet away to talk, leaving Brodie, Sam, and Cam alone.

They watched August draw Kyla into their first dance together as a married couple. The way his mother looked up at him, her eyes gleaming with joy, produced mixed feelings for Cam. He knew she'd always love his father, but he was gone. She deserved happiness.

What clutched at his heart was how their being together signaled the final end to her first marriage. Cam would never feel for another man what he had for his father. Seeing August whirl her around the floor, he knew it was time to put it all behind him and concentrate on his future with Vangie.

"When will you be moving Jean-Paul to the Northern California Mental Asylum?" Between the trial and work at the ranch, Cam hadn't kept up with what was decided about the gypsy.

Brodie took a sip of his already fortified punch. After several meetings and the recommendation of Doc Vickery, August had ruled him incompetent to stand trial. Given he was also considered a menace to society, there'd been one choice. He'd be sent to the large hospital closer to the coast.

"Next week. The lad admitted to shooting Thane, robbing the bank, and killing his partner. We found Turner's body right where Jean-Paul left it. The old gypsy woman we'd been holding finally confirmed what he'd done."

"We're pretty certain he's the one who shot at you and Vangie," Sam said.

Cam held out his punch for Brodie to pour a little of his whiskey into the glass. "Aye. We've had no problems since he was arrested. How long will the lad be there?"

"The rest of his life," Sam answered.

When the band began a lively tune, several of the MacLarens grabbed their wives for the traditional Scottish reel. Not wanting to be left out, Cam, Brodie, and Sam moved to the women, inserting themselves onto the dance floor.

As they whirled around to the music, laughing with each step, Cam couldn't help feeling an unbreakable bond of love for his family.

He'd been blessed and he knew it. All of them did. There was nothing he wouldn't do for any one of them, and he knew they felt the same about him. Soon, Vangie would join the tight-knit clan, giving Cam everything he'd ever wanted.

In this small section of land were all the people he loved. Blaine, Lia, Caleb, and Heather had made the trip from Settlers Valley. And they'd do it again in a month.

Whether celebrating or facing a threat, they came together, asking no questions, protecting each other. All the cousins still had younger brothers and sisters who'd join those older than them to continue the tradition. Plus, there were the children who'd been born in the last few years. And more would come.

Right now, all Cam wanted to think about was what he had and his future with Vangie. Life could never get any better than this.

Thank you for taking the time to read Cam's Hope. If you enjoyed it, please consider telling your friends or posting a short review. Word of mouth is an author's best friend and much appreciated.

Watch for my other books on all online retailers.

If you want in on all the backstage action of my historical westerns, join my VIP Readers Group.

Join my Newsletter to be notified of Pre-Orders and New Releases:
https://www.shirleendavies.com/

I care about quality, so if you find something in error, please contact me via email at
shirleen@shirleendavies.com

About the Author

Shirleen Davies writes romance. She is the best-selling author of books in the romantic suspense, military romance, historical western romance, and contemporary western romance genres. Shirleen grew up in Southern California, attended Oregon State University, and has degrees from San Diego State University and the University of Maryland. Her passion is writing emotionally charged stories of flawed people who find redemption through love and acceptance. She lives with her husband in a beautiful town in northern Arizona.

I love to hear from my readers!

Send me an email: shirleen@shirleendavies.com
Visit my Website: www.shirleendavies.com
Sign up to be notified of New Releases:
www.shirleendavies.com
Check out all of my Books:
www.shirleendavies.com/books.html
Comment on my Blog:
www.shirleendavies.com/blog.html
Follow me on Amazon:
http://www.amazon.com/author/shirleendavies
Follow my on BookBub:
https://www.bookbub.com/authors/shirleen-davies

Other ways to connect with me:

Facebook Author Page:
http://www.facebook.com/shirleendaviesauthor
Twitter: www.twitter.com/shirleendavies
Pinterest: http://pinterest.com/shirleendavies
Instagram:
https://www.instagram.com/shirleendavies_author
/

Books by Shirleen Davies

Historical Western Romance Series

MacLarens of Fire Mountain

Tougher than the Rest, Book One
Faster than the Rest, Book Two
Harder than the Rest, Book Three
Stronger than the Rest, Book Four
Deadlier than the Rest, Book Five
Wilder than the Rest, Book Six

Redemption Mountain

Redemption's Edge, Book One
Wildfire Creek, Book Two
Sunrise Ridge, Book Three
Dixie Moon, Book Four
Survivor Pass, Book Five
Promise Trail, Book Six
Deep River, Book Seven
Courage Canyon, Book Eight
Forsaken Falls, Book Nine
Solitude Gorge, Book Ten
Rogue Rapids, Book Eleven
Angel Peak, Book Twelve
Restless Wind, Book Thirteen
Storm Summit, Book Fourteen, Coming next in the
series!

MacLarens of Boundary Mountain

Colin's Quest, Book One,
Brodie's Gamble, Book Two
Quinn's Honor, Book Three
Sam's Legacy, Book Four
Heather's Choice, Book Five
Nate's Destiny, Book Six
Blaine's Wager, Book Seven
Fletcher's Pride, Book Eight
Bay's Desire, Book Nine
Cam's Hope, Book Ten

Romantic Suspense

Eternal Brethren, Military Romantic Suspense

Steadfast, Book One
Shattered, Book Two
Haunted, Book Three
Untamed, Book Four
Devoted, Book Five
Faithful, Book Six, Coming Next in the Series!

Peregrine Bay, Romantic Suspense

Reclaiming Love, Book One
Our Kind of Love, Book Two
Edge of Love, Coming Next in the Series!

Contemporary Romance Series

MacLarens of Fire Mountain

Second Summer, Book One
Hard Landing, Book Two
One More Day, Book Three
All Your Nights, Book Four
Always Love You, Book Five
Hearts Don't Lie, Book Six
No Getting Over You, Book Seven
'Til the Sun Comes Up, Book Eight
Foolish Heart, Book Nine

Burnt River

Thorn's Journey
Del's Choice
Boone's Surrender

The best way to stay in touch is to subscribe to my newsletter. Go to www.shirleendavies.com and subscribe in the box at the top of the right column that asks for your email. You'll be notified of new books before they are released, have chances to win great prizes, and receive other subscriber-only specials.

Copyright © 2019 by Shirleen Davies

For permission requests, contact the publisher.

Avalanche Ranch Press, LLC
PO Box 12618
Prescott, AZ 86304

Made in the USA
Columbia, SC
20 January 2021

31337732R00163